VIVA GRINGO!

U.S. Marshal Ezra Macahan picks the wrong time to visit his cavalry soldier brother, Joshua, at Camp Furlong, New Mexico. That night Pancho Villa and his revolutionary forces raid the town of Columbus and though defeated, one of Villa's commanders, 'Scar' Acosta, kidnaps Joshua's son, Daniel — and flees to a heavily guarded mountain hideout. But, as Ezra and Joshua pursue Daniel's captor, they ever rescue him when they face terrible adversities, a shocking revelation and violent death?

Books by Steve Hayes
in the Linford Western Library:

GUN FOR REVENGE

STEVE HAYES

◆

VIVA GRINGO!

Complete and Unabridged

LINFORD
Leicester

First published in Great Britain in 2011

First Linford Edition
published 2011

British Library CIP Data

Hayes, Steve.
 Viva gringo!. - -
 (Linford western library)
 1. Western stories.
 2. Large type books.
 I. Title II. Series
 823.9′2–dc22

 ISBN 978–1–44480–625–0

Published by
F. A. Thorpe (Publishing)
Anstey, Leicestershire

Set by Words & Graphics Ltd.
Anstey, Leicestershire
Printed and bound in Great Britain by
T. J. International Ltd., Padstow, Cornwall

This book is printed on acid-free paper

For my wonderful sisters
Elfreda and Joyce

BOOK ONE

1

He was sitting at an old plank table on the patio of the cantina, sopping up the last of his refried beans with a tortilla when he saw them ride in. For a moment he thought it might be the noon day heat playing tricks with his eyes. But no, it was the Colson gang all right. Their faces were burned into his memory.

Macahan almost laughed. For six grueling weeks he had been tracking them through the sun-baked canyons and across the scrub-covered plains below the foothills of the Sierra Madre Occidental, never getting closer than the cold ashes of their camp fires and now, when he had almost reached his limit, here they were, all three of them, joking around, riding right into his lap.

Stuffing the bean-soaked tortilla into his mouth, he grabbed his Winchester

'94 and ducked behind a crumbling adobe wall. Flies buzzed persistently in his face, attracted by the bean juice clinging to the graying stubble around his lips. He brushed them aside, wiped the juice away with his sleeve, and concentrated on the three riders.

They came closer. He could now see the trail grime on their sweaty faces; the snuff stains yellowing their beards; the bulges under their dirty shirts made by belly-guns.

A burst of giggling laughter made him look to his right. Across the dirt street in an alley filled with trash three grubby half-naked children were tormenting a scrawny ginger kitten. The kitten kept trying to escape and the children kept pulling it back by its tail. Its pitiful mewing was hidden by the children's laughter. Macahan cursed their presence and prayed they wouldn't run into the line of fire. Years ago while shooting it out with two drunken gunmen in El Paso a ricocheting bullet had killed a little girl. No one ever proved whose bullet it was but her death continued to haunt him.

Footsteps behind him made him glance over his shoulder. The fat, hair-lipped barkeep stood watching him from the cantina doorway.

Macahan signaled to him to stay put. '*Tres bandidos americanos.*'

The barkeep nodded to show he understood, and crouched behind the bar. Macahan could see the man's reflection in the tilted back-bar mirror and thought the top of his bald head looked like a brown mushroom.

Resting his rifle atop the wall, Macahan trained his sights on the lead rider and waited. Sweat dripped from his brow into his eyes. It stung, and not wanting to make any big movements that might be seen by the gunmen, he kept his hands down and blinked several times until he could see clearly again.

The three men, big men with hard surly faces wearing sweat-stained Stetsons and soiled tan dusters that hid the pistols holstered on their hips, eased up their lathered horses as they reached the main street of the dusty little pueblo. The leader, a hulking, red-bearded hard case named Riles Colson, thumbed at the cantina and signaled for the others to follow him.

Macahan watched them approaching through his sights. Should he give them a chance to surrender or gun them down now? Either way he had earned his wages — plus a reward offered by the El Paso Bankers' Association. These men were border trash, outlaws wanted for a dozen killings, bank robberies and rustling — so why risk his neck when no one would blame him for shooting them in cold blood?

His finger curled around the trigger. All he had to do was squeeze off three shots and he would not only still be alive but a thousand dollars richer. But he was no bushwhacker. Damn fool, he thought as he relaxed his trigger finger. One day, your conscience is going to buy you a pine box.

In front of him the outlaws had dismounted and were tying up their horses.

'Hold it right there,' he said, showing himself.

Startled, the outlaws froze. Then Colson, recognizing Macahan, laughed and spat out his chew. 'You in Mexico, Marshal. Your badge don't mean squat down here.'

'But the warrant in my pocket does. It's signed by the governor of Chihuahua.'

It was a lie, but it worked.

Colson lost his smirk and went for his gun.

Before he cleared leather, Macahan shot him in the heart. Colson stumbled back with a choking cry and collapsed in the dirt.

Macahan levered another shell into the chamber and aimed his rifle at the other two outlaws. The oldest, Rafe McIntyre, already had his gun out and Macahan pumped two rounds into him. Without pausing, he swung the Winchester onto the last man, a thin gawky boy no more than seventeen, and shot him before realizing he was raising his hands in surrender.

It was over in seconds.

The children, startled by the gunfire, saw the three gringos sprawled in the street and came running over to rob them. The boy holding the kitten by the tail was the last one out of the alley. As he ran the kitten mewed and tried to scratch him. The boy swung it against the cantina wall. The kitten went limp and stopped fighting. The boy kneeled beside his friends and started picking the outlaws' pockets.

'Get out of here!' Macahan yelled. He shook his fist at the children. '*¡Largate! ¡Me oistes! ¡Largate!*'

The children grudgingly retreated to the alley and watched, waiting for Macahan to leave so they could strip the boots from the bodies.

Stepping into the street, he cautiously approached Colson's corpse. He prodded it with his boot. The outlaw's head lolled sideways, his blank-staring eyes indicating he was dead. Macahan did the same to McIntyre. He was dead, too. But the boy wasn't. He lay on his back, teeth gritted, hands clutching the hole in his belly as his life-blood slowly oozed from him.

'H-Hurts,' he said.

Macahan didn't answer.

'What you shoot me for? W-Wasn't going for my iron . . . '

'Neither was the bank guard you shot in El Paso.'

'That weren't me.'

'Witnesses say it was.'

'They's wrong. It was Rafe done the shooting. Only man I ever killed was trying to gut me with a pig-sticker.'

Macahan shrugged. 'Keeping tabs ain't up to me, sonny.'

The boy closed his eyes and grimaced with pain. His breathing grew shallow and blood trickled from the corner of his mouth. He worked his lips with great effort. 'I done some right sorry things in my life but I ain't never shot no fella with his hands up. That's

9

the Amen t-truth.'

'It's not high on my list neither.'

'But you ain't sheddin' no tears over it?'

'Not over the likes of you.'

'H-Hope you rot in hell.'

'Reckon that's a foregone conclusion.'

High overhead buzzards were already circling. One swooped low over the cantina, its shadow slanting across the yellow tattered awning that fluttered in the hot dry wind like flags of defeat.

'I need me a d-doctor,' the boy said.

'Closest one is two day's ride from here. You'd never make it.'

'I could try.'

'No point. Just lifting you onto your horse would kill you.'

'I don't get no goddamn doctor, I'm goin' to die anyways.'

'Won't argue that.'

The boy coughed up more blood. He wheezed and his face turned gray. 'You one mean, c-cold son of a bitch, Marshal.'

'Won't argue that, neither.'

'Finish me off then.'

'Nope.'

'It's the least you can do. P-Please,' he said when Macahan didn't answer. 'I'm hurtin' awful bad.'

'Don't whine, boy. Dignity's the way.'

'Y-You'd shoot a horse if it was sufferin', wouldn't you?'

Macahan heaved a sigh. Hunkering down beside the boy he looked deep into his wide blue eyes. He saw no fear, just pain, lots of lingering pain, and rising he aimed between those blue eyes and pulled the trigger.

It was a tough way to earn a thousand dollars.

2

He had rolled the three corpses up in their blankets and tied them facedown over their saddles when he heard horses approaching — lots of horses. So many, he could feel the sun-scorched earth trembling underfoot.

He looked down the rutted clay street that ran between two rows of adobe hovels and saw the families living in them come out and look off toward the desert. Whatever they saw made them gesture excitedly.

Macahan grew uneasy. The *Revolucion Mexicana* was in its sixth year now and the American-backed troops of President Carranza had driven the Villistas out of every state except this one. Here, in Chihuahua, Villa still ruled and Macahan guessed that the approaching horses were part of his cavalry; perhaps even his trusted

Dorados, the Golden Ones.

Knowing how unpredictable Villa could be toward gringos, especially since his inglorious defeat by the Carrancistas at Agua Prieta, Macahan led the outlaws' horses into the alley alongside the cantina. There, his rangy piebald mare, Lady, stood dozing at the rail outside the kitchen door. Untying her, he stepped into the saddle and kicked her into a trot. The alley angled into a narrow dirt street of white-washed adobe houses that ended at a sunny tree-lined plaza. Macahan rode across the plaza, watched by curious storekeepers from their shady door-ways. Living within two days' ride of the border they were used to seeing gringos riding through, but seldom one leading three horses carrying corpses; especially corpses dripping blood.

Macahan kept his hand near his Colt in case someone challenged him. No one did. He left the plaza, following a gully that served as a street, and quickly reached the outskirts. The last building was a recently renovated white Spanish church, *San Juan de Dios*. He cantered through a cool spear of shade formed by the bell tower and on, past a group of white-shirted *campesinos* working in a field, until he was safely out of Janos. Ahead, a plain of sunburned grass sloped up into the rocky brown foothills. Beyond the hills rose the distant rugged peaks of the Sierra Madre.

Macahan looked back. The cluster of adobe buildings still hid his view of the approaching horsemen, but the noise of the hooves now sounded like rolling thunder. It was definitely time to make tracks. He spurred the piebald mare toward the hills.

Halfway there an ugly thought struck him: a lot of blood had been spilled outside the cantina. If — no, *when* the Villistas saw it, they might be curious about what happened. When the bartender gave them the details, how would they react? Would they shrug it off as just another gringo shootout or would they want to know who the gringo was and send men after him?

Deciding not to take any chances, Macahan angled off to his left and rode into a shallow pebble-bottomed creek that crossed the plain in front of the hills. Slowing the mare to a walk, he kept to the shallows. The blood dripping from the blood-soaked blankets turned the water crimson. Silvery minnows darted after the droplets, thinking they were blood worms.

After a few hundred yards, Macahan looked back at the corpses and saw that the blankets had almost stopped dripping. Guiding the horses ashore, he spurred the mare once more toward the hills. His ploy wouldn't fool the Villistas if they were persistent, but hopefully they had more important things to do and wouldn't consider him worth following.

Once hidden among the hilltop rocks, Macahan focused his field glasses on the horsemen riding into the far end of the pueblo. Despite the dust swirling around them, he estimated there were about one hundred riders. Most of them wore white shirts crisscrossed by their signature bandoliers, high-crowned sombreros, sashes around their waists and baggy trousers. Some were armed with old bolt-action Mauser rifles supplied by the Germans, who were trying to turn Mexico against the U.S.; but most carried repeating Model '73 Winchesters sold to them by American gun-runners. Pistols flopped on their hips and many of them had machetes slung over their backs. All were mounted on small, sturdy horses and rode as if born in the saddle. Riding with them were several *soldaderas*, tough, loyal, vigorous women who fought alongside their men in the revolution.

Surprised to see so many Villistas this close to the border, Macahan shifted his glasses to the front of the untidy column and looked for a familiar face among the officers. But Francisco 'Pancho' Villa was not present. Instead they were led by a small, slim, mustachioed man of forty in a dark-blue tunic with brass buttons and khaki pants tucked into high brown boots. He rode a purebred dappled-gray horse and sat arrogantly erect on a fancy hand-tooled saddle decorated with silver conchos. His sombrero was pushed back off his head, and Macahan recognized him instantly by the long white scar that puckered his left cheek. Known as *La Marcada Uno*, The Scarred One, Manuel Diego Acosta was Villa's most ruthless commander.

Lowering his glasses, Macahan pulled his hat down low to shield his eyes from the glaring sun. An uneasy thought struck him. Before he'd left El Paso, he'd heard rumors that Villa was so angry at the U.S. for transporting Carranza's troops by train to Agua Prieta, then supplying the electricity for searchlights that made his attacking Villistas easy targets for Carrancista bullets, he was planning to retaliate by raiding the border towns. Few, if any, actually believed he would. Audacious as Villa was, to attack U.S. territory would be suicidal. The government in Washington had already shown its disdain for the colorful former *bandito* by endorsing his bitter rival, Venustiano Carranza. Also, there were camps and forts along the border and a well-trained garrison at Ft. Bliss, El Paso, under General John Pershing's command that could easily crush Villa's ragtag army.

Still, there was no denying that this was a formidable force, and as Macahan watched the Villistas massing in the pueblo, he could not help feeling uneasy about so many fighting men within striking distance of his homeland.

3

Once he had assured himself that the Villistas were not interested in who had been shot, or pursuing him, Macahan rode through the hills at a steady, easy lope until he had put several miles between himself and the pueblo. By then it was late afternoon and he had reached a shallow bend in the *Rio Casas Grandes*. After resting long enough to water the horses and smoke a cigar, he forded the tree-lined river and rode northeast until dark.

He made camp in a secluded arroyo guarded on three sides by wind-sculptured rocks. Rather than hobble the outlaws' horses, he blocked the narrow entrance with a barricade of dead, sun-bleached creosote bushes. Then loosening their cinches but leaving the blanket-covered corpses tied over their saddles, he fed each horse a handful of grain. Lastly, he unsaddled the patient piebald mare, gave her the last of the grain and watered her from his canteen. Lady nudged him appreciatively with her muzzle. But the moment he turned his back, she lowered her head and tried to open his saddle bags with her teeth. Macahan shouldered her aside, 'Whoa, wait, hold your horses, dammit,' and squatted beside the bags. Lady cocked her head at him, as if amused by the absurdity of his remark, and impatiently pawed the dirt until he dug out a coffee can. Quickly, she tried to grab it with her mouth. But he was ready for her and roughly elbowed her aside.

'Goddammit, be patient, will you?' Prying open the lid, he tipped a few ground coffee beans into his palm and offered them to the mare. Lady wrinkled back her lips, licked up the sticky grains, snickered happily and nudged him for more.

'Uh-uh, that's all you get.' He pushed her away. But she was not having any of it and followed him like a lost puppy as he collected enough mesquite and dry grass to build a small fire. Exasperated, he got out his hobbles and dangled them in front of her. Lady whinnied and backed up; stood there glaring at him. Macahan ignored her. Emptying his canteen into an old blackened coffee pot, he heated the water over the fire and then filled his enamel mug with muddy-looking coffee. The mare angrily stamped her foreleg but made no attempt to move closer.

Macahan stretched his long legs out on his bedroll, leaned back against his saddle and ate the last of his jerky and hardtack. The hardtack was stale and he dunked it into his coffee until it was soft enough not to break his teeth. When he was finished eating he rolled a smoke and lit it with a burning stick. A bitter wind off the Sierras made him shiver. He wrapped his serape around him to keep out the damp chill. Cold was his enemy: it caused the arthritis in his left shoulder to flare up. Once it started, the stabbing ache kept him awake all night. A doctor in El Paso whom he'd consulted about it told him it was incurable and would only get worse as he got older. Depressed, Macahan left the office feeling he had wasted his money and from then on avoided the cold at all costs.

Just before bedding down, he threw the coffee dregs on the ground by the piebald. Lady tossed her head indifferently and didn't move. Macahan chuckled and crawled into his blankets. The last noise he remembered hearing before falling asleep was the mare slurping up the coffee-soaked sand.

*   *   *

He rose early the next morning. The pre-dawn gray sky was streaked with primrose and mauve and a light mist whitened the hilltops. Pulling on his boots he stamped the numbness from his feet, saddled up and rode at the same steady mile-consuming lope toward the border.

By mid-morning he was only a few miles south of Palomas, the port of entry into the United States. Reining up in a narrow *barranca*, he dismounted to relieve himself and to give the horses a rest. But he had barely re-buttoned his Levi's and lit his last cigar when the mare whinnied nervously. Moving to the rim of the gully he peered over the top and saw a cloud of swirling dust approaching from the southwest. Still more than a mile away, it was undoubtedly caused by a large number of riders.

He got out his field glasses. It took a moment to focus then a column of mounted Villistas appeared. There were at least three hundred of them. They were all armed, all traditionally dressed, all led by a middle-aged man on a white horse. Burly, swarthy, and sporting a thick black mustache, he wore a tan tunic-style jacket, white shirt, a yellow bandanna tied loosely at his throat, and a plain flat-brimmed brown hat.

Knowing he was looking at Pancho Villa, Macahan quickly returned the glasses to his saddle bag, mounted, grabbed the reins of the outlaws' horses and kicked the piebald into a brisk canter. He kept to the gully for as long as it lasted. When it finally became too narrow, he was forced to ride on level open ground exposing himself to the Villistas. He hoped to get a jump on them but they spotted him immediately. About a dozen of them left the column and spurred their mounts in his direction.

They came across the desert at an angle, rapidly closing ground, and Macahan realized they intended to kill or capture him. Alone on the piebald he would not have been concerned; Lady could outrun most horses. But the outlaws' mounts balked at being pulled along and fought their bits, jerking their heads, tugging at the reins and slowing the mare down.

Puffs of smoke appeared as the Villistas opened fire. Their aim was poor and the bullets whined past him, ricocheting off the rocks. But with Palomas still a mile off and his pursuers quickly gaining ground, Macahan knew it was merely a matter of time before he was hit. He looked about him, hoping to spot a place where he could hide the horses and the bodies then double back later for them and still collect the reward. But the land was flat and he knew he would not reach Palomas before the Villistas rode him down. Cursing his bad luck, he reluctantly released the reins of the outlaws' horses and spurred the mare into a full gallop.

At once his pursuers stopped gaining on him. Ahead, in the distance, he now saw the scattered adobe dwellings of Palomas. He breathed easier. Unless there were more Villistas waiting for him in the quiet little pueblo he was home free.

Just then the mare lurched and almost stumbled. Macahan jerked her head up and Lady quickly regained her stride and galloped on. Guessing she had stepped in a rut or a gopher hole, he leaned low over the mare's neck and encouraged her onward. She gamely obliged and within minutes he was close enough to the village to see the curious brown faces of its inhabitants watching him from their doorways.

He glanced over his shoulder. The Villistas had given up the chase and were riding back to the column. Relieved, Machan eased the mare up and fondly patted her on the neck. Her hide was sweaty and flecked with foamy spittle. He wiped his hand on his thigh and was shocked to see blood on his Levi's. He reined up immediately, dismounted and looked the mare over. Blood ran from her mouth and, with a grunt, Lady sank to her knees. Macahan kneeled beside her and saw blood welling from a bullet hole just behind his left stirrup.

'Jesus,' he said.

The mare wheezed loudly and tried to get up. But her legs betrayed her. She lay there, motionless, fighting for air as her lungs filled with blood.

Macahan took her head between his hands and held it gently. The big blue eye nearest him stared back. It was filled with so much trust he could have wept.

'Damn you,' he said softly. 'Who's going to share my coffee with me now?'

The unwinking blue eye stared at him for another moment. Then it closed and the mare shuddered. Her head became a dead weight in his hands. He knew she was gone. He lowered her head to the warm sun-baked dirt and got to his feet. His world had suddenly become a lonelier, darker place. He turned to several small, half-naked urchins who had come running up and now stood watching him. Not one of them was over ten but he spoke as if they were men. '*Tienen que cuidar mi caballo. ¡Cuiden me caballos con sus vidas!*'

'*Si, señor.*'

'*No dejen que nadie la toquen. Nadie! ¡Me entendien!*'

'*Si, señor.*'

'*Yo llegade pronto. Dile que el Cabacho va matar al que toquen mi caballo!*' Satisfied that they understood he would be back shortly and that they must guard the dead mare with their lives he dug out some coins and shared them among the children. Instantly, as if by drawn by an invisible magnet, other children came running up demanding pesos. Macahan ignored them and walked grimly into the village.

* * *

The border guard stepped from his gate-shack and held up his hand to the tall, lean, tight-lipped man driving the two-wheeled ox-cart toward him. A new recruit, he was anxious to prove to his superiors that he could handle the job.

'Mister, you can't bring that dead horse across.'

'Her name's Lady.'

'What?'

28

'She was born in the U.S. of A.'

'I don't care if she was born in the White House and related to Abe Lincoln, you ain't bringing no fly-bitten carcass across on my watch.'

'Reckon you'll have to shoot me to stop me.'

The guard looked uneasy but stood his ground. 'If I got to, I will.'

'Be gunning down a Deputy U.S. Marshal.'

'Got any proof of that?'

Macahan opened his fringed leather jacket and showed the badge pinned to the lining. 'Name's Macahan. Ezra Macahan. Out of El Paso.'

The border guard frowned. 'There's a Corporal Macahan stationed up the road at Camp Furlong. You a relative?'

'Joshua's my kid brother. He's quartered off-base in Columbus. Wife's name is Celia. His son's Daniel.'

'How about Lieutenant Zachary Macahan?'

'He's kin, too. But I ain't seen him since he deserted.'

That seemed to satisfy the border guard. 'I reckon you're who you say you are, Marshal. But I still don't know about that dead horse.'

'Better jerk your iron then, son, 'cause I'm coming through.'

'Marshal, it's against the law to bring dead animals — '

'She saved my life and I ain't leaving her in this hell hole to end up in somebody's enchiladas!'

The border guard wilted. Without saying 'pass' or 'don't pass,' he went back inside his shack and looked in the other direction.

Macahan took the hint and snapped the reins, The oxen plodded ahead, accompanied by a swarm of flies, and the cart carrying the dead mare slowly rolled through the gate into the U.S.

4

After about three miles along the Deming-Guzman wagon road he reached Camp Furlong, home of the 13th Cavalry. Unfenced and sprawling, the camp was separated from the dingy little town of Columbus by the El Paso and Southwestern Railroad tracks. Macahan left the rutted clay road and drove the ox-cart up to the sentry patrolling the western perimeter. Showing the young soldier his badge, he said he had an urgent message for Colonel Slocum.

The sentry dragged his gaze from the dead piebald and pointed past a row of military tents to a small, tin-roofed, adobe-brick building that stood alone on a dirt mound. 'You'll find the C.O. in there, Marshal.'

Thanking him, Macahan drove the cart between the flimsy wooden barracks and open stable sheds, on past the armory and pulled up outside company headquarters, Every soldier he passed looked questioningly at the dead mare then at him, all trying to figure out why this grim-faced, stone-eyed lawman was bringing a dead horse to their commanding officer.

The sentry outside headquarters recognized Macahan. He started to greet him then suddenly broke off and saluted as Colonel Herbert J. Slocum emerged with the duty officer. Both stopped abruptly as they saw Macahan and the dead horse and for a moment neither seemed to know what to say. Finally the Colonel, a tall, erect, crusty man in his sixties with a trim white mustache, told the duty officer to carry on and offered his hand to Macahan. 'Hello, Mac, This is a surprise. What brings you to Columbus? Official business or your brother's furlough?'

'I'll stop by and see Josh 'fore I leave,' Macahan said. 'But he ain't the reason I'm here.' He explained that he'd just ridden up from Casas Grandes and while passing through Janos had spotted a column of Villistas.

'Who were they led by?'

'*La Marcada Uno.*'

'So, Scar has finally left his stronghold.'

'That'd be my guess.'

'Was Villa with him?'

'No. But he was with another column I ran into south of Palomas.'

Colonel Slocum sighed and stroked his mustache. 'Another alleged sighting. By God, I swear I'm getting two or three every day. Trouble is, they're all ambiguous and contradictory. Villa's here, there, and everywhere it seems.'

'This sighting wasn't 'ambiguous,' Colonel, or 'alleged.' It was one of Villa's greasers who shot my horse. What's more, I figure the reason they chased me was they weren't happy about being seen so close to the border and wanted to stop me from reporting them.'

Colonel Slocum frowned, troubled. 'Including the men with Scar, how many Villistas do you think there were altogether?'

'Close to five hundred.'

'That's more men than I have under my command.'

'That's why I figured you ought to know.'

'Of course my boys are better trained and better armed, and certainly more disciplined. We also have artillery and machine guns. Nevertheless, it would be a sizable force to contend with — especially since they have the element of surprise.'

'Not if you send out scouts.'

'That's just it, Macahan. I can't. Orders direct from Washington forbid me from sending scouts into Mexico.'

'Why would they tell you a damn fool thing like that?'

'President Carranza considers any foreign intrusion into his country a threat.'

'To hell with Carranza. He's just another corrupt cutthroat, like all the rest.'

34

'My sentiments exactly. However, according to General Pershing, Carranza has persuaded our president to side with him. So what can I do?' He brushed a horse fly from his neck. 'But I appreciate your taking the time to warn me. I'll certainly mention it to my staff. Now, is there anything I can do for you?'

'I could sorely use a shovel.'

'Sign one out at the quartermaster's. Oh, and if you need a horse, you can sign for that, too, at the stables.'

'Mighty obliged to you, Colonel.'

★ ★ ★

Opposite the little yellow train station, across the Deming-Guzman road, was a low scrub-covered rise called Cootes Hill. Macahan chose the west slope facing the mountains known as *Tres Hermanas*, so the venerable Three Sisters could watch over Lady, and toiled in the hot sun until he had dug a hole big enough for the mare. If he had broken the piebald's legs, like most gravediggers did with horses, he would not have needed to dig such a large hole. But he felt Lady deserved better and after burying her, he said a short prayer and covered the grave with rocks. He then drove the ox-cart back across the border and left it beside a leathery old man snoozing under a straw sombrero by the gate.

'Ain't you going to wake him?' the border guard said.

'He'll wake when he's ready.'

'What if someone tries to steal the team?'

'Shoot 'em. It'll make up for not shooting me.' Ignoring the ugly look the border guard gave him, Macahan untied the bay gelding from the rear of the cart and rode back through the gate.

* * *

On reaching Columbus, he did not go to his brother's off-base quarters but turned onto Broadway Street and guided his bay toward the Hoover Hotel.

As he rode between the wood-fronted stores and scattered adobe and clapboard houses, he noticed the tiny desert town was even more sparsely populated than usual. The reason did not dawn on him for a moment; then it hit him: there were no Mexicans! Normally, they made up two-thirds of the five hundred residents. Yet today, as he glanced around, he saw very few. And those he did see avoided his gaze and quickly hurried out of his way as if they did not want to be near him.

It made him uneasy. Was their absence related to all the Villistas he'd seen? And if so, what did they know that no one else did? Hoping his brother could answer his questions, he reined up in front of the Hoover — a rectangular two-story adobe hotel with a flat roof, narrow oblong windows and a wooden upstairs balcony jutting out over the front door. Macahan dismounted, tied the bay to the hitch-rail, and carried his saddle bags inside.

The Hoover was one of only two hotels in town. The other, the Commercial, was owned by Sam Ravel, a businessman who allegedly had sold guns and ammo to Villa. The Commercial was bigger and had more amenities than the two-story adobe Hoover, and up until four years ago Macahan always stayed there whenever he was in town. Then one day the only woman he had ever loved, a fine-looking, capricious Irish woman with flame-red hair and the unlikely name of Prudence, got tired of waiting for him to propose, and took off. He expected her to return, as she had always done before, but she didn't. She packed everything up and moved away, telling no one where she went, and he never saw her again.

Losing her left a hole in his heart that he knew would never heal. And the Commercial Hotel, where they had enjoyed their idyllic tryst, became a painful reminder of his stubborn resistance to marriage. He never stayed there again.

Now, as he signed the register and collected his room key from the desk clerk — a big Nordic-looking woman named Martha — he forced himself to forget about Prudence and asked what had happened to all the Mexicans.

'Happened?'

'I didn't see none around.'

'Oh, sure . . . yeah . . . been that way for a couple of days now.'

'Any notion why?'

'Uh-uh. Some say it's because Villa's planning to attack us. But I don't hold much stock in them kind of rumors. I mean, why would Villa shoot his own people? He's trying to win their support against Carranza and you don't get a lot of votes from dead folks.' She laughed at her own joke then added: 'Also, he ain't likely to raid us with Camp Furlong right on our doorstep.'

Macahan's room was on the second floor at the end of the hall. It was small, clean, spartanly furnished and smelled of stale cigars. It had a window facing Broadway and the bank opposite. If he leaned close to the glass and craned his neck he could see along the cross street, East Boundary. Bordered by a few scattered shacks the street ran string-straight out into the desert. Lowering the blind, Macahan stripped down to his long johns, washed the trail dirt from his face and hands and climbed between the cool clean sheets. He stretched luxuriously, sighing as his aches gradually disappeared. When he had been younger and hard-bellied, sleeping on the ground wrapped in a blanket under the stars hadn't seemed like such a hardship; now, pushing fifty, he was certain of one thing: heaven was a soft bed with clean sheets. He yawned. Suddenly he was dead tired. He closed his eyes and fell asleep, thinking about how lucky his kid brother was to have a beautiful loving wife and a fine son to take fishing and hunting.

5

It was early evening when he next awoke. He would liked to have rolled over and gone back to sleep, but he was taking the train back to El Paso in the morning and did not want to leave without seeing Joshua and his family.

Rising, Macahan turned up the kerosene lamp on the bedside table. His shadow appeared on the wall, copying every move he made. He amused himself for a few minutes making hand-shadows of different wild birds. At the same time he whistled, imitating their various unique calls. It was something he only did when he was alone as the image of a Federal lawman being interested in birds was not one he wanted to portray to the public; and especially not to outlaws and gunfighters he needed to intimidate by his mere presence.

Completing his repertoire, he went to the chest-of-drawers, lifted the pitcher and poured water into the chipped porcelain basin. The water was rust-colored and sediment swirled at the bottom. He hesitated, momentarily reluctant to splash it on his face; then deciding he would most likely die from a bullet long before rusty water killed him, he washed the sleep from his eyes and dried off on the towel draped over a nail behind the door.

Refreshed, he stretched the stiffness from in his back, raised the blind and looked out the window. Dusk had settled in. There was no electricity in Columbus and without a moon or street lights it was already dark outside. The stores and cafes were closed. And since the residents prided themselves on being God-fearing teetotalers, there were no cantinas to brighten up the night. There was a jail, though. A light glimmered in the little oblong adobe building and Macahan guessed the deputy was finishing up his paperwork.

Across the street, beyond the bank, oil lamps glowed in the windows of the houses. Families he couldn't see were sitting down to supper. Hungry himself, he suddenly felt lonely and wondered what Prudence was doing at that moment; was she having supper with her husband and young'uns?

Instantly, he cursed himself for reminiscing. There was no place in the life of a lawman for dime-novel sentimentality. Just ask that boy he shot yesterday, the boy who was trying to surrender and had called him a mean, cold-hearted son of a bitch: see what he thought about sentimentality.

There was a faint tapping behind him. Macahan turned and saw a Miller moth hurling itself repeatedly against the glass protecting the lamp-wick. He tried to cup his hand around the moth, but it kept escaping. He persisted and, finally, the exhausted moth flew into the flame. Its pale, speckled brown wings flared for an instant and then it fell, dead. So much for good deeds!

Opening his saddle bags, Macahan took out a worn-only-once plaid shirt he had bought at Hanoran's Haberdashery in El Paso. Shaking out the wrinkles, he buttoned it on, added a string-tie and his lucky silver horseshoe clasp and looked at himself in the mirror. A man older than his years stared back at him. Damn! Who was the fool who said graying temples made a man look distinguished? And when the hell did his once-thick brown hair start receding? Those squint-lines cornering his pebble-gray eyes did not help either; nor did the jowls that were beginning to destroy his jaw line, giving him a slightly hangdog expression. Christ, no wonder attractive women now treated him as if he were invisible.

Buckling on his gun belt, Macahan pulled on his fringed leather jacket and his black, flat-brimmed Stetson, wiped the dust from his boots on the edge of the bed cover, and went out.

★　★　★

When he emerged from the hotel he momentarily looked around for the piebald mare. She was not at the hitch-rail and for a second he wondered if she had been stolen. Then remembering she was dead, he glumly stepped into the saddle and kneed the bay gelding along East Boundary. The dark street was deserted. The post office on his left was closed. But a few doors farther north lights glowed in Colonel Slocum's house, suggesting Camp Furlong's commander was tucked in for the night.

Macahan rode on, comforted by the muffled *thud-thudding* of the bay's hooves on the sandy dirt. Insects whined about his ears. He slapped them away and reached for his cigars. He was out and he chided himself for not buying some at the hotel desk. Ahead, silhouettes suddenly loomed up. As he got closer they became a cluster of small clapboard homes. He tried to remember which house was his brother's. It had been more than a year since he had seen Joshua and in the inky darkness he rode past it.

'Out for an evening ride, Marshal?'

Macahan reined up, hand instinctively dropping to his six-gun. But the voice was familiar and friendly, and relaxing he turned the bay around. A shadowy figure sat on a stump in front of a brown house. A match flared in cupped hands, the flame lighting a readyroll and illuminating his younger brother's tanned, boyish, grinning face.

'Lucky for you I just happened to be sitting out here or you might've ridden clear on up to Deming.'

Macahan chuckled, dismounted, and tied the bay to a withered clump of mesquite. 'Who says Deming ain't where I'm headed?'

'Colonel Slocum, for one.'

'Talking to the big brass now, huh? I'm impressed.'

'Don't be. He didn't speak to me directly. Colonels don't stoop to talk to lowly corporals; especially corporals who refuse promotions. It's beneath them. But apparently he thinks enough of you, big brother, to have his aide ride over and tell me you were coming. Lucky thing he did, too. Or you'd be in Deming and I would've never known you were here.'

'Well, if you'd live in a halfway decent berg, one with electricity and running water for instance, maybe a fella wouldn't need a sniffin' dog to find you.'

The brothers Macahan laughed and hugged each other warmly.

'Dammit, *hermano*, it's powerful good to see you.'

'You too, Ez. Been way too long.' Joshua stepped back, blonder, shorter but broader and thicker through the chest than his brother. 'Sorry to hear about Lady. I know how you felt about her.'

Macahan nodded sadly. 'She wasn't the best piece of horseflesh I ever saddled, but she was a gamer who never quit, and I'll miss her.'

'Understandable. Had her quite a spell, didn't you?'

'Broke her in just after Daniel was born.'

'Eight years? My God, where'd all the time go?'

'Beats me. But you don't look none the worse for it.'

'That's Army life for you.'

'Now you sound like one of them gung-ho recruiters.'

'Ha! That'll be the day.' Joshua grinned. 'Hell, you know me, Ezra. I was born lazy. But for Celia pushing me all the time I'd probably spend my life eating and sleeping and obeying orders. But she won't stand for it. She runs roughshod over me whenever I slack off or try and bury my head in the sand, or don't fight for what I want — '

The front door suddenly opened bathing them in warm yellow light. A tall, boyishly-slim, fiery young Mexican woman stood silhouetted against the lamplight behind her. Her long black hair was tied back with a pale green ribbon that matched her off-the-shoulder dress; she had smooth tawny skin and lovely shoulders that curved up into a neck as graceful as any swan's. But none of that mattered compared to her flashing dark eyes and full, kissable red lips.

'*Dios Mio*, are you two going to stand out here forever?' Her low throaty voice was pleasing and despite her Spanish heritage, thanks to private tutors she did not have a trace of an accent.

'Calm down, woman, we'll be right in,' Joshua said.

'*Bueno*. I will tell Daniel to wash his hands while I put dinner on the table.' She smiled at Macahan. '*Buenas noches*, Ezra. *¿Como estas?*'

'Not bad for these decrepit old bones.'

'Ha! You'll outlive us all.' Celia stood on tiptoe and kissed his stubbly cheek. 'It is wonderful to see you again.'

Macahan, as always when he saw her and smelled her lavender scent, felt twenty years slide off him. 'Run away with me, *hermosa senora*.'

'*¿Cuando?*'

'*En seguida.*'

'Hey, you two,' said Joshua. 'I'm right here, you know. I can hear every word you're saying.'

They ignored him and continued flirting.

'*¿Que tal mi marido?*' Celia said.

'*Olividese de el. El perro no se merece usted.*'

'What the hell you doing?' Joshua asked his brother.

'Stealing your wife. What's it sound like?'

'Couldn't you do that without referring to me as a dog?'

Macahan chuckled. 'It was the least offensive slur I could think of.'

'Thanks. Next time come right out and ask me if you can have her. My answer might surprise you.'

'I doubt it, *hermano*. I ain't been surprised since she was fool enough to get hitched to you.' He winked at Celia. 'Come, *señora*,' he picked her up as if she were weightless. '*Estamos perdiendo un tiempo precioso.*'

'Time's not the only thing you're wasting,' Joshua said. 'There's a little matter of supper. Can't you two lovebirds at least wait until after we've eaten before you run off?'

'My husband does have a point,' Celia said. 'And I do hate to see a fine meal go to waste.'

'After supper it is,' Macahan said. He brushed past his brother and carried Celia into the house.

6

That night while they were enjoying a savory meal of chili-chicken, rice and vegetables, Macahan told Joshua about his run-in with the Villistas. He also mentioned how few Mexicans seemed to be in town and wondered if it had anything to do with the rumored attack by Villa. Josh did not disagree but said he had not noticed any fewer Mexicans around. But he was not the right person to ask, he added. Since he had started his furlough two days ago he'd barely left the house. He then asked his wife if she'd noticed any Mexicans leaving for the border in the last few days. Before she could answer, Daniel said: 'I have, Uncle Ezra.'

'You have?' said Celia. 'Why didn't you mention it?'

Daniel shrugged. He was a beautiful boy; so beautiful he would have made a better girl. He had his mother's dark hair and huge, expressive dark eyes, long curling lashes that every girl envied, and a sunny disposition not unlike his father's. Admittedly, he was short for his age, especially considering how tall his father and uncles were; but no one seemed to be worried: he would shoot up later, they assured Celia and Joshua, probably when he was in his teens.

'I didn't think it was important,' he said.

'Well, next time you notice anything around here that's unusual, you be sure to tell me. Understand?'

'Yes, Momma.'

Celia turned to Joshua. '*Is* it important?'

'I don't know. Could be, I reckon. If Ez, here, is right, it could mean the greasers are clearing out so they won't get hit by any stray bullets.'

'Greasers?'

'Sorry. That's the Army talking. Mexicans.'

'Then you actually believe Villa is going to attack Columbus?'

'I didn't say that. Truthfully, I've no idea.'

'What about Colonel Slocum and his staff?'

'What about them?'

'They haven't mentioned anything to you?'

'Oh, sure, every morning at staff meetings.'

'There's no need to be sarcastic, I was merely asking.'

'Sorry. It's just that no officer tells me anything, other than what to do. Hell, they'd sooner spit into the wind.'

'Maybe it's time you became an officer then — so you'd be one of them and know what's going on.'

'I don't want to be an officer.'

'Not even a general?' Daniel said.

' 'Specially not a general.'

'Why not? Generals get to lead charges and have long, shiny sabers and — '

' — Earn lots money and don't have

to clean out latrines,' Celia said.

'They're also responsible for sending men into battle.'

'What's so bad about that?' Daniel said. 'All you got to do is ride a white horse and yell 'charge!''

Joshua rolled his eyes and turned to his brother. 'You tell them, Ez. Maybe coming from you they'll understand.'

Macahan finished rolling a smoke, licked the paper, sealed the edge, and stuck the cigarette between his lips. 'I'm not sure I understand myself.'

'Traitor. You're supposed to be on my side.' Joshua finished his bourbon and refilled his glass from a bottle. 'For the last time,' he said to Celia and Daniel, 'I don't want to be an officer 'cause I don't want to be responsible for ordering men to their death.'

'Not everyone dies in battle.'

'No, some are lucky enough to just get their arms and legs blown off or their guts spilled out or to just lose an eye or spend their autumn years suffering from shell shock — '

'*Madre de Dios*,' said Celia. '*No enfrente del nino.*'

'Why not?' Joshua said. 'Daniel has a right to know why his dad won't be an officer.' He leaned close to his son, adding: 'Maybe that sounds cowardly, and if it does then maybe I am a coward. It takes brave men to go into a battle knowing they might get killed or wounded, but it also takes brave men to send them. Men that know at the end of the day they have to count their losses and watch the wounded being carted off and the dead being buried, and it's all because they gave the order. And it doesn't end there. Tomorrow they have to do it all over again. Order more men to go off and die or get wounded. And tomorrow and tomorrow and tomorrow after that . . . In fact for as long as wars exist and people want to kill each other — which is most likely forever.'

'Joshua Macahan, that's enough!'

For once he ignored his wife and cupped his hands about Daniel's sweet oval face. 'Do you understand what I'm telling you, son — why I don't want to be an officer?'

Daniel, his eyes shiny dark saucers in the lamplight, looked at his mother then back at his father, undecided. 'I don't know. Maybe. But . . . '

'But what, son?'

'Are you saying you'd sooner get killed or wounded than give orders?'

'Yes. Though in truth, I'd sooner do neither.'

'Then why'd you become a soldier?'

'Good question, son.' Joshua looked at his brother, smoking silently across the table from him. 'That's why I took this furlough: so I'd have a couple of weeks to figure out if I wanted to stay in the Army.'

★   ★   ★

When it was time to leave, Macahan crept into Daniel's bedroom, slipped a silver dollar under his pillow, kissed his sleeping nephew goodbye, and then joined Joshua on the front porch. There in the cold, misty darkness they stood smoking in silence save for the high-pitched whine of insects and the *yip-yipping* of distant coyotes.

'Celia's really pissed at me,' Joshua said finally. ' — in case you hadn't noticed.'

'She'll get over it.'

'Don't count on it. You know how stubborn she can be. Once she gets an idea set in her mind, it takes a goddamn miracle to shake it loose.'

Macahan chuckled. 'Seems like I remember you telling me that this was what you liked about her: her fire and passion. How she stood up for herself no matter what.'

'I did. Still do.'

'Then what's eating at you?'

Joshua hesitated, as if unwilling to discuss it, and then said: 'I hate to disappoint her. And right now I think she's more disappointed than angry.'

'I doubt that. She loves you too much to care if you're an officer or not.'

'I'm not so sure. Besides being feisty, she's got a mountain of pride. Wants me to be the best I can be no matter what it takes.'

'No crime in that.'

Joshua wasn't listening. 'She gets that trait from her father — along with her temper. I never met him, of course. Huerta executed him before I met Celia. But friends of his, old dons who came to the house, they told me that other than Celia, who was the joy of his life, the only two things that really mattered to him were pride and integrity.' Joshua paused and flicked his readyroll off into the darkness, a trailing rainbow of sparks arcing to the ground. 'That's why he continued to speak out and write articles against Huerta; said the people deserved better than a despot who ruled by fear, corruption and assassination.'

Macahan didn't say anything.

'Celia adored him. Even now she talks about him like he was some kind of great revolutionary martyr.'

'Wasn't he?'

'I reckon.' Joshua rubbed his nose with his fist. 'I know Celia wishes I was more like him — '

'She tell you that?'

'Not in those exact words. But I'd have to be a damn fool not to know what she's thinking.' He laughed cynically. ''Lonely is the man who reads between the lines.''

'Who said that?'

'You don't remember?'

'Reckon not.'

'Zach.'

'Zach?'

'We were riding back from El Paso late one night on the Drunkard's Special. As usual everyone was either drinking or passed out. I'd had too many beers and was trying to get some sleep. Zach kept talking and talking about women, you know like he does some times, and I said — well, I forget exactly what it was I said but it had something to do with what goes through a fella's mind after he's bedded

60

a woman . . . and Zach, he laughed and got this strange, sad look in his eyes, as if he was picturing himself in the same situation. Then he said, like he was quoting someone: 'Lonely is the man who reads between the lines.' I must have looked puzzled because he suddenly laughed, you know, the way he does when he's mocking you, and slapped me on the back. 'Cheer up, *hermano*,' he said. 'I was just pulling your leg.'

'But you don't reckon he was?'

'I know he wasn't. That's the sorry thing about it. He sounded like the loneliest man in the world.' His voice trailed off and for a few moments. Neither brother spoke. Somewhere far off a lonely coyote yipped. One of its cousins answered and for a few moments the night was filled with their yowling.

'I don't blame her,' Joshua said presently. 'Celia, I mean. For thinking so highly of her dad. Truth is, I admire him myself. Hell's bells, they say he was still cursing Huerta while he was standing in front of the firing squad.'

Macahan didn't say anything.

'I wish I could be that brave.'

'*Doo nidahilldzidgo da.*'

'What's that? Apache lingo for brave?'

'They call it 'Being without fear.''

'Then I wish I was without fear.'

'The Apaches also say that a man without fear is his own worst enemy.'

'Sounds like they're hedging their bets, as Zach used to say.'

'They're like proverbs: you dig deep enough you can always find one that contradicts another.'

Joshua nodded, and gave a troubled sigh.

'If something's chewing at you, *hermano*, now would be a good time to spit it out.'

'It's that obvious, huh?' Joshua grinned ruefully. 'Reckon I never was much good at hiding my feelings.' He lit another readyroll before continuing. 'Look, I know we promised never to bring this up, but have you heard anything about . . . Zach?'

'Nary a word.'

'You'd tell me if you had, right?'

'Got my oath on it.'

'I wish I knew where he was, Ez. Hell, I don't even know if he's alive or dead.'

'He's alive,' Macahan said.

'You just saying that or do you know for sure?'

'If he was dead, we would've heard something. Mexico's big in space but small when it comes to gossip. A dead gringo deserter couldn't be kept secret too long.'

'But what if Zach isn't in Mexico anymore? What if he sneaked back across the border and is living here somewhere?'

Before Macahan could reply, the door opened and Celia stepped out in her nightgown. Both men turned and faced her.

'I'm going to bed now, gentlemen. So I'll say goodnight.'

Macahan reached out and hugged her. 'Sleep tight, *mujer hermosa*. And thanks for a fine supper.'

'*De nada*. I am just glad you came by to see Josh.'

'He didn't come by to see me,' Joshua said. 'In case you haven't noticed, woman, it's you he's in love with.'

'Is that true?' Celia said, smiling. 'Are you in love with me, Ezra Macahan?'

'Up to my saddle sores,' he said.

'Men,' Celia laughed. 'You are all so hopelessly romantic.'

7

Gunshots and shouting startled him awake. Instantly alert, Macahan struck a match and looked at his fob watch on the bedside table. It was almost eleven minutes after four in the morning. The gunfire increased. Grabbing his Colt from the holster hanging on the bedpost, he went to the window.

Outside, without a moon, it was so dark he could not see the attackers; only the flashes from their rifles. But by the number of flashes he knew it was a large force and before long he began to make out a swarm of shadowy figures advancing toward the center of town. Sporadic gunfire came from the houses as the townspeople fired back. But they were scared and badly out-numbered and Macahan knew their paltry efforts would not drive back the raiders.

Raising the window, he stuck his

head out. He could hear yelling and more gunfire in other parts of town. The attack was being launched from both southeast and southwest. There was also heavy gunfire coming from across the railroad tracks in Camp Furlong. Macahan guessed the troops had been surprised by the attack but were now grimly fighting back.

Cursing the darkness, he looked along Broadway and gradually the shadowy shapes materialized into several hundred Villistas charging toward him. Most kept to the street but others fanned out and began breaking into the scattered homes. Shots were fired. Macahan heard women screaming. He realized it was more a mob than an army. With their high-crowned sombreros bobbing on their backs, the Villistas fired indiscriminately into the houses and stores on both sides of the street and shot anyone who tried to stop them. As they got nearer, Macahan could hear them shouting: '¡Viva Villa! ¡Viva Villa!'

Others joined in.

'*¡Muerte a los gringos!*

'*Adelante, muchachos! Adelante!*'

'*Mexico siempre!*'

Macahan grimly pulled his head back in. Pulling on his clothes, he stepped into his boots, buckled on his gun-belt and grabbed his rifle before running from the room.

Downstairs, the panicked guests were huddled in the lobby. Martha was trying to calm them. When Macahan came running downstairs, she grabbed his arm and begged him to stay and protect them.

'Dammit, woman, protect yourself. All of you,' he added to the frightened guests. 'Arm yourselves. Grab whatever weapons you can and start shooting at those greasers!'

'Yes, yes,' one man agreed. 'We must fight back!'

'With *what*?' said an older man. 'I have no weapon. What am I supposed to use, my fists?'

'My rifle's up in my room,' said the

first man. 'I'll get it.'

'Yes, and I have a shotgun in the office,' Martha said. 'You can use that.' She hurried off.

Macahan pushed out the door and ducked behind one of the posts supporting the balcony. Though it was still dark, he could now plainly see the Villistas swarming toward him. Their crackling gunfire filled the night.

As he pumped bullets into the onrushing Mexicans, he wondered if Joshua and his family were safe. He considered making a run for their house, but the attackers were closing in on two sides and he was pinned down by their bullets. Dammit, where was the goddamn army?

Rifle fire now came from behind the walls of the bank opposite. Macahan couldn't see the shooters, but he heard people yelling that Villa was after the money in the safe and they must defend it at all costs.

Their stiff resistance slowed down the attackers. These men were not Villa's famous, once-powerful *Division del Norte*: disciplined, well-mounted cavalry that had crushed Huerta's Federals at Zacatecas, men committed to follow their leader to their death; they were peasants, eager but un-trained volunteers who had been captivated by Villa's bombastic rhetoric and left their farms and pueblos with outdated weapons and little or no experience in battle. Nor were the hastily promoted officers leading them much better. They wilted under the withering gunfire and, had it not been for their superior numbers, would have retreated.

Even so, the Villistas kept pressing forward, jumping over their fallen comrades and continuing to yell encouragement to one another.

Macahan realized it was only a matter of minutes before he and the others were overwhelmed. Two of the hotel guests began firing from the windows. The Villistas returned fire. Their barrage of bullets chipped holes in the adobe wall and wounded one of the shooters. He staggered back with a cry, but his determined companion kept shooting.

A block west, on Main Street, flames appeared above the rooftops. Someone hiding behind the bank shouted that the Villistas had looted the Commerical Hotel then set fire to it. Within moments the raging fire spread to some of the nearby shacks and soon the night was bright with flames.

Macahan again cursed the absence of the Army.

But ironically, the fire turned the tide. Now able to clearly see their enemy, the townspeople fired on the Villistas with renewed determination, and began driving them back.

Outside the Hoover, Macahan could also distinguish his targets. He picked off two Mexicans who had crawled close and then shot the officer who had been encouraging his men onward. As he reloaded his Winchester, Macahan saw a small detachment of U.S. cavalrymen fighting their way through the Villistas. Hemmed in on all sides, the machine gun troop was led by an officer he recognized: Lt. James Castleman.

Relieved to see them, Macahan pumped shot after shot into the Villistas battling the soldiers. The Mexicans fell back, allowing the troopers to break through to the hotel.

There was no time for greetings. Signaling his thanks to Macahan, Lt. Castleman ordered his men to set up the French-designed Benet-Mercie on the corner outside the hotel. Meanwhile, Macahan and the rest of the troop protected them with withering cover fire. The two men handling the 'Ben-A,' as the troopers called it, quickly spread the bipod, slid a clip in, then turned the gun on the advancing Villistas.

The forward ranks were mowed down, the bodies piling up so fast the men following stumbled over them. The charge faltered. But within moments the flawed, temperamental machine gun jammed and the Villistas charged forward again.

A second machine gun troop burst

out of a side street. Led by Lt. John Lucas, they set up their Ben-A on the corner of East Boundary and opened fire. Again the charge faltered. Luckily, this gun didn't jam and before the Villistas could recover, the first machine gun was back in action, catching the Mexicans in a deadly cross-fire.

The battle turned into a slaughter. Panicking, the Villistas quickly fell back. The machine guns continued to cut them down. The retreat quickly became a headlong flight. Cheering, the cavalrymen pursued them, firing as they ran, adding to the burgeoning number of casualties.

The threat to the bank over, Macahan left the townspeople to mop up any stragglers and ran along East Boundary to his brother's house. Between buildings, he glimpsed the Commercial Hotel. It was engulfed in flames and as he continued on, he felt a strange mixture of relief and regret, knowing that his connection to Prudence would soon be nothing but ashes.

8

He reached Joshua's house in minutes. The door had been battered off its hinges and three dead Villistas lay outside. Heart in mouth, Macahan rushed indoors and saw his brother lying face-down on the floor, a carbine beside him. Blood seeped from a wound on the back of his head. Rolling him over, Macahan checked Joshua's pulse. It beat strongly and, knowing his brother would live, he ran into the bedroom. It was empty. Though the bed had been slept in, there was no sign of a struggle. Macahan hurried on into the adjoining bedroom where Daniel slept. It too was empty. But the covers were in disarray, as if the boy had been dragged from the bed. An alarmed Macahan hurried back to his brother.

Joshua, still groggy, was slowly getting to his feet.

'What happened?' Macahan said. 'Where's Celia and the boy?'

Joshua stared blankly at him, mind in a fog.

Macahan gripped him by the shoulders and repeated his question.

'H-He took them,' Joshua said. 'I . . . I tried to stop him, but . . . '

'Stop who?'

'Acosta . . . '

'Manuel Acosta — Scar?'

'Yeah. I shot two or three of 'em . . . his men, I mean . . . but the others . . . one clubbed me with his rifle and . . . I don't remember much else except . . . hearing Celia scream . . . then everything went — '

'Stay here!'

'Wait,' Joshua said, grabbing his brother's arm. 'Where're you going?'

'See if I can catch up with them.'

'I'll go with you.'

'No, you'll slow me down.'

'I don't care. I'm going.' As both men ran to the door, Celia came rushing in. She was distraught. Her nightgown was torn and filthy from being dragged in the dirt and there were bloody scratches on her face. She staggered and would have fallen if Macahan hadn't caught her and kept her upright.

'H-He's got Daniel,' she sobbed.

'Scar, you mean?'

She nodded, half out of her mind, and suddenly grabbed Macahan by his shirt. 'I begged him to let Daniel go, but he only laughed in my face.'

'Don't worry. I'll bring him back.'

'Sure, sure,' Joshua said. 'We'll get Daniel back in no time.'

'Did Scar say anything about a ransom?' Macahan said.

Celia shook her head. 'I told him I'd pay whatever he wanted, but he just laughed and rode away.'

'Dirty little greaser, I'll kill him when I get my hands on him. C'mon, Ezra!' Joshua started for the door, but his legs gave out and he collapsed.

'Get him to the doc',' Macahan told Celia. 'Most likely he's got a concussion.'

Joshua pushed their hands away. 'N-No, I'm fine. Fine. I'm just . . . ' Halfway to his feet he collapsed again, and this time couldn't get up.

'I'll take care of him,' Celia told Macahan. 'Just go!'

He went.

* * *

Macahan ran to the little corral behind the house. He could hear sporadic shooting as townspeople and soldiers mopped up the retreating Villista stragglers. The heaviest gunfire came from the direction of Cootes Hill. The predawn sky was still lit up by the blazing remains of the Commerical Hotel, and when Macahan reached the corral he saw a chunky, muscular dun nervously pacing inside. It had a gold body, black mane and tail, and a dark stripe down the middle of its back. Macahan knew the horse belonged to Celia, and remembered its name was Oro.

Grabbing a rope halter hanging over the fence, he opened the gate and slowly approached the dun. It backed up suspiciously. He called it by name and spoke soothingly to it. When he had it calmed, he looped the halter over its head, fed the bit into its mouth and, keeping hold of the end of the rope, swung up onto the dun's back. It cow-kicked but made no attempt to buck, and Macahan easily guided it out of the gate. Kicking it up into a gallop he rode toward the railroad tracks, cutting between houses and across vacant lots until he reached the Deming road. From here he could see cavalry-men gathered atop Cootes Hill, firing after the retreating Villistas. The sky was growing paler by the minute. A few miles behind Macahan, magenta and lilac streaks showed above the peaks of the Florida Mountains.

He urged the dun halfway up the hill. He could now see Colonel Slocum bravely standing on the crest as he issued commands to his men. Most of them lay prone as they fired into the Villistas, who were making a lastditch stand about five hundred yards south of the railroad tracks.

Macahan could not see the Mexicans' faces clearly. He doubted that Villa or Scar would be with them now that the raid had failed, but had to be sure. Descending the hill, he rode alongside the wire border fence until he reached the gate-shack. It was empty. The gate had been broken open and Macahan eased the dun through it, and rode east.

After twenty minutes or so, he reined up. He was now behind the Villistas who were still falling back under the cavalrymen's fire. Wishing he had his field glasses, Macahan nudged the dun forward until he was within sixty or seventy yards of them. Most of them were now mounted and firing from the saddle. Macahan checked out the horses and could not see Scar's dappled gray among them. Satisfied, he wheeled the dun around, and galloped back to

Columbus. Rage consumed him. He would find Acosta. Find him and kill the no-good kidnapping son of a hitch and bring Daniel home no matter if it took him the rest of his life.

9

It was shortly after dawn when Macahan, now astride the bay, rode into Camp Furlong. All the fires in town had been put out, but the smell of smoke was everywhere. Dismounting at the stables, he made his way to the wood-frame hospital. The severely wounded soldiers had been tended to by the surgeon, and now the men with minor wounds stood waiting in line, smoking and talking to one other about the raid.

From their conversations Macahan learned that a detachment led by Major Tompkins was pursuing the Villistas into Mexico. The pursuit was in violation of the U.S. Army's rules of engagement, they said, but it had Colonel Slocum's blessing. Macahan, after listening to the soldiers and having met the major, had no doubt he would make the raiders pay heavily.

Joshua now emerged from the hospital and joined his brother. His head was bandaged but his eyes were clear and he seemed back to normal. He frowned, surprised to see Macahan. What was he doing there? Had he found Daniel or Acosta or — ? Macahan stopped him and briefly explained what had happened. He added that he was leaving for Mexico as soon as he wired the U.S. Marshal's office and took care of a few things, and would not return without Daniel.

'I'm going with you.'

'Be better if you didn't.'

'Don't give me that. He's my son, Ez. I couldn't get through a single day if I had to sit around wondering if he was dead or alive.'

'He's alive.'

'You don't know that.'

'No reason for him not to be. Scar took Daniel for ransom, I'd bet my life on that. And he knows damn well if anything happens to the boy, he'll not only lose his money but end up dancing from a rope.'

'But what if he demands more than I can rustle up?'

'Doesn't matter. You ain't paying him no matter what he asks.'

'But — '

'Josh, the only hope we got of keeping Daniel alive is to make Scar think we're going to pay and, in the meantime, find him and kill him 'fore he can do the boy harm.'

'Okay, but I'm still going, I already told Celia when she brought me here that I intended to ask the Old Man to extend my leave. And if he won't play along then I'll just go AWOL and take my chances when I get back. Now, how soon can we leave?'

'Soon as I fill my list.'

'List?'

'Of everything we'll need. This won't be no picnic. Scar has a small army of followers, most of them willing to bite the bullet for him, and if we're to get past 'em and rescue Daniel we better be loaded for bear. Now,' he said as he put his arm around his brother's shoulders, 'let's you and me go talk to the Colonel. Work out some kind of arrangement that don't land you in the stockade or force you to go AWOL. One goddamn deserter in the family is more than enough.'

★ ★ ★

Colonel Slocum beat them to the punch. He sent his aide to find them and when Macahan and Joshua entered company headquarters and stood before his desk, they knew by his scowl that he did not have good news.

'I'll come right to the point, gentlemen: I've arrested your brother.'

'Zachary? My God, when, sir?'

'A short time ago.'

'Is he wounded?' Macahan said.

'Few scratches, is all. His horse was shot out from under him during the raid and he was captured with several other Villistas. He was mistaken for one of them at first, but then Sergeant Cantrell recognized him and brought it to my attention — '

'Where is he, Colonel?'

'Presently he's being detained, along with the other Villista prisoners, in the Columbus jail. But once the military paperwork is complete and he's been officially charged, he'll be transferred to a military prison to await sentencing.' The colonel paused, cleared his throat and smoothed his mustache. 'Naturally he'll be court-martialed and then, in all likelihood, executed.'

'For deserting?'

'No, Marshal, Treason.'

Macahan and Joshua exchanged grim looks.

'That's a mighty harsh accusation.'

'Sir, Zach's no traitor,' blurted Joshua.

'That's for a military tribunal to decide. But I'm sure you're aware that it is considered treason for a citizen of the United States to bear arms against his own country.'

'Zach was fighting for the Villistas?'

Joshua looked shocked. 'I can't believe that, sir.'

'Nevertheless, it's true. Part of Villa's army consists of mercenaries. They're outcasts and deserters mostly, from here and Europe, similar to the kind of murderous riffraff that join France's Foreign Legion — '

'*Falange extranjero*,' Macahan said quietly.

'Yes, I believe that's what they call themselves.'

'And Zach's one of them?' Joshua said.

'Yes. Has been for over a year.'

Macahan expelled his breath in a long troubled sigh. 'I'd like to see him, Colonel.'

'That's your prerogative, Marshal. But you should know he is listed as just another Villista prisoner. I would like it kept that way. In fact I insist you do not tell anyone who he is or that Lt. Macahan's your brother.'

'Why, sir? What's — ?'

'Corporal, I would think that was

obvious. The people of Columbus are riled up at the moment and if they thought one of their own was involved in the burning and looting — well, I fear they'd try to lynch him.'

'They'll have to go through me first,' Macahan said.

'And me, sir,' said Joshua.

'Yes, well, be that as it may, I do not need to contend with any more violence. So for the moment I insist you keep this between us. Now, is there anything else you wish to speak to me about?'

'Yes, sir,' Joshua said.

'It'll keep,' Macahan interrupted. 'Good day, Colonel.' He steered his brother out of company headquarters and away from the sentry before stopping.

'Why the hell did you drag me out like that?' Joshua said. 'I thought you wanted me to talk to the Old Man right away?'

'That was before I heard Zach had been arrested for treason. Jesus on the cross, the way the Colonel's feeling about the Macahan family right now you couldn't buy a favor from him if you offered him a goddamn four-star promotion.'

10

The Columbus jail stood on a patch of sunburned dirt on the corner of Lima and Main. A yellow, single-story, oblong adobe building no bigger than a shack, it had small barred windows all around and only one door made out of iron. Sitting, smoking, in the shade outside the door was Deputy Sheriff Jack Thomas, a tough, lean, laconic man whose uncle was the famous U.S. marshal, Heck Thomas, of Indian Territory.

He got up from his chair as Macahan and Joshua dismounted and tied their horses to the hitch-rail. 'Afternoon, Marshal.'

'Deputy . . . ' Macahan shook Thomas's calloused hand. 'Reckon you know my brother, Josh.'

'Nope, never had the pleasure.' The two men shook hands. 'What brings you to my door?'

'I need to speak to one of the prisoners.'

'Sure, Which one?'

'The gringo.'

Deputy Thomas couldn't hide his disgust. 'That pig-suckin' bastard. Did you know he was fighting alongside the greasers?'

'Not till a few moments ago.'

'It just don't figure. A man white as you'n me turning against his own country to fight for a bunch of chili farters.'

Joshua reddened and angrily started to say something. But Macahan silenced him with a nudge. 'Whys and wherefores,' he said. 'They seldom make sense. Now, how about opening up, Deputy?'

'Sure. But only one of you can go in at a time. And I got to lock the door after you.'

'You going to talk it open or use a key?' Macahan said.

Deputy Thomas flushed, but something in the marshal's cold gray eyes warned him to keep his mouth shut.

Macahan handed his Colt .45 to Joshua while the deputy unlocked the padlock and slid aside the bolt. The door swung open and a foul stench hit Macahan in the face.

Deputy Sheriff Thomas spat disgustedly. 'Like I said: chili farters.' He waited for Macahan to step inside then slid the bolt shut behind him.

Macahan stood by the door, waiting for his eyes to grow accustomed to the gloomy light. He had never been in the jail before and, when he could see properly, he realized the only furniture was a small desk and a rickety wooden chair that matched the one the deputy had been sitting on outside.

The rear half of the room consisted of two cells divided by iron bars. In one, several Villistas sat glumly on the dirt floor, backs against the wall, arms around their drawn-up knees, heads covered by sombreros. They all looked up as Macahan entered, then as he ignored them, went back to sleep.

Macahan approached the other cell.

Inside, the man slumped down next to the bars was dressed like a Villista. But despite his darkly tanned skin and Zapata-style mustache, his curly sandy hair and blue eyes suggested he was not Mexican. He did not look up as Macahan stopped beside him but he did glance at the lawman's boots.

'Times must be rough, Marshal.'

'Times are always rough.'

'I was referring to your boots. You could use a new pair.'

Macahan looked at his shabby, scuffed, worn-heel boots. 'Just got these broken in to how I like them.'

The man, still without looking up, poked his hand through the bars. Macahan hunkered down and gave him his half-smoked cigarette. The man took a deep drag and exhaled the smoke with a satisfied sigh.

'Do you know what Zapata once told me? Said in Mexico folks judge a man by his boots.'

'That's because most times they intend to shoot him for them.'

The man chuckled. 'Come to watch the hanging, did you?'

'I'd sooner hear your side of the story.'

'There is no 'my' side. I'm an American deserter who took up arms against my fellow citizens. Simple as that.'

'Treason's never simple.' Macahan took a readyroll from his shirt pocket, scratched a match on the bars and fired the cigarette.

The man looked at Macahan for the first time. Other than both being tall, there was little resemblance between the two brothers. Zachary was blond, slender, and as handsome as Byron. His eyes were periwinkle blue and, like his smile, filled with mocking impudence. He had a poet's way with words, which women found enchanting, and a cultured voice tainted with snobbery. 'Never thought I'd see the day when the famous Marshal Macahan would give up handmades.'

'I ain't give them up. Got this from Josh.'

'Ah, yes, Joshua. How is our beloved young sibling?'

'Feeling betrayed right now.'

'I can imagine. He always was idealistic.'

'Patriotic, not idealistic.'

'How can a West Point graduate become a traitor?'

'You can see how it might bother him some.'

'It's his own fault. I never asked him to put me on a pedestal.'

'Wasn't a choice. You're his older brother.'

'So are you. But no one expected *you* to be a role model.'

'I done my best.'

'On your own volition; not because you were pressured into it.'

One of the Villistas in the adjoining cell began to snore. Another farted.

'Charming, aren't they?' Zachary Zebulon Macahan said.

'You chose to fight with 'em.'

'Indeed I did.'

'Why was that? Care to share?'

'Money, what else?'

'You had money.'

'Lieutenant's pay? I'm afraid my indulgent tastes go way beyond that. Besides, I got tired of all the dreadful rules and regulations. Ignorant martinet officers. Inferiors for superiors.'

'So why not just serve your time and walk away?'

'Avoid a court-martial at any cost?'

'Not a bad thing.'

Zachary mulled over his brother's words. 'I considered it. But due process would have taken too long. By then I'd already had it up to *here*.' He indicated his nose. 'I needed to leave immediately.'

'So you ran out like a coward.'

'If you're trying to shame me, forget it. I'm guilty as charged. Look,' he said as he crushed his butt on the dirt floor, 'I'm sorry I disgraced you and the family name. I know how much it means to you being the son of a decorated Civil War general. But, I'm just not officer material. I don't have the spine for it. Or the discipline. Or the character. Neither does Josh, by the way. 'Least, not when I last saw him.'

'Leave Josh out of this.'

'Ah, A tad sensitive about our baby brother, are we?'

'He's a good man. Just needs to straighten out his brains.'

'And his backbone — which no doubt his Mexican firebrand will help him do.'

'Nothing wrong with a stand-up woman.'

'Especially if you fancy her for yourself.'

Stung, Macahan instinctively reached for his Colt. When he realized he was unarmed, he stared stony-eyed at his brother.

Zachary laughed. 'You don't think I would have said that if you'd been packing a weapon, do you?'

'Hard to tell. You're a lot of things, most of which I don't like, but I'd never peg you for a coward.'

'Why, thank you, Ezra. Coming from

you, that's a true compliment. But back to Josh and the military. As I tried to tell father many times: if he was going to send one of us to the Point, it should have been you.'

'I didn't have the schoolin'.'

'I know. And that's the rub. You would have made us all proud.'

'I like to think I done that anyway.'

'You have, brother mine. You've accomplished everything a father would want his son to be. Why, thanks to you, the illustrious Macahan name is still synonymous with law, honor, and integrity.'

'I see you ain't lost none of your sarcasm.'

'Oscar Wilde preferred to call it 'biting wit.''

'Who?'

'Just someone I've been reading lately. Riding around Chihuahua with a bunch of illiterate tortilla-eaters is not only incredibly boring, it tends to lower one's self-esteem, not to mention intelligence.'

Macahan sighed. 'Why is it whenever we talk, I feel like we ain't speaking the same language.'

Zachary chuckled, started to say something sarcastic then suddenly lost all his gaiety and became grimly sober. Gripping the bars with both hands, he pressed his face between them and apologized to his older brother. 'By God, Ezra, I'm sorry. Sorrier than you'll ever know.'

Macahan just stared at him.

'I've let you down — you and Josh — and it's eating my guts out. I don't expect you to believe this — I surely wouldn't in your shoes — but I'd do anything to make it up to you.'

Macahan looked into his brother's startlingly blue eyes and saw nothing but sincerity. 'There might be a way.'

'Speak.'

Macahan lit his last two readyrolls, gave one to Zachary, took a drag off his own and then explained how Manuel Acosta had kidnapped Daniel and taken him to Mexico. Though he hadn't asked for any ransom yet, Macahan believed that money was Scar's reason for snatching the boy and was sure Celia or Joshua would soon receive a note demanding payment. In the meantime, Macahan intended to go after Acosta and try to rescue Daniel. But he had no idea where Scar had taken him. So if Zachary knew or could even guess where he might be — '

'I don't have to guess. I know exactly where he'd take Daniel: to his stronghold. What's more I'll be happy to take you there. I always hated that arrogant little son of a bitch. He thinks he's Mexico's answer to Napoleon.'

Macahan took out a stubby pencil and a little dog-eared notebook and offered them to his brother. 'Make a map showing where Scar's stronghold is.'

'Uh-uh. No maps.'

'Meaning?'

'You want the location — you get me out of here.'

'Get you — ? How am I supposed to

do that? Colonel Slocum's got you dead to rights. It'd take a presidential pardon to clear you of treason.'

'Then get one.'

'You know I can't.'

'Try. Otherwise, you'll have to find Daniel yourself.'

'You ain't serious?'

'Oh, but I am. Deadly serious.'

'But Daniel's life most likely depends on us finding him quick.'

'All the more reason for you not to spend weeks, maybe months, roaming aimlessly around Chihuahua looking for him. It would not only be a waste of time, it would be life-threatening to Daniel.'

'Tell me something I don't know.'

'About Acosta, I could tell you plenty. You may know him as a sadistic bastard, but that isn't the half of it. Believe me, I know first hand. Son of a bitch is ten times more vicious and unpredictable than Villa. If he doesn't get his ransom quickly, he's likely to change his mind and send you a box filled with Daniel's remains.'

'You know that, and yet you can still refuse to help us?'

'Damn right. I only have a few weeks at most to live. And you're the only person standing between me and the gallows. So quit trying to appeal to my conscience — which doesn't exist any more — and use your influence to get me out of here. Otherwise, say *adios* to our nephew.'

Macahan went white. 'If I had a gun right now, I swear I'd blow a goddamn hole through you.'

'You'd be doing me a favor, *hermano*. Anything's better than hanging.' Zachary turned away from his older brother and sat on the floor with his back to the bars.

11

Outside, Macahan took Joshua aside and told him the bad news. Joshua couldn't believe it. Surely Ezra was mistaken. Zachary loved Daniel. He must have told him and Celia that a thousand times. How could he now risk his nephew's life by making such impossible demands?

Macahan shrugged and said he didn't know. But he sensed Zachary had changed; grown harder, more cynical. Macahan had no idea why. All he knew after talking to him was that this wasn't the lovable, fun-loving hell-raiser either of them had grown up with. Agreed, Zach had always had a habit of putting himself ahead of others, his brothers and parents included, but never like this. Hell's fire, before talking to Zach Macahan would have bet his life that his brother would help them.

'I'll talk to him,' Joshua said. 'I don't give a damn how close he is to hanging, the son of a gun won't be able to look me in the eye and refuse to tell me where Daniel is.'

But a little later, when Joshua came storming out of the jail, Macahan did not need to ask him how it went. Grinding his smoke out under his heel, he mounted up and together he and his brother rode across the border to the nearest cantina and drowned their rage and frustration in tequila. Macahan soon realized that was a mistake. Lost in his own anger, he had forgotten his brother couldn't hold his liquor and as a result wasn't prepared when, after their third drink, Joshua turned belligerent. Pounding his fists on the bar, he said he was going home to get his .45, and then march on over to the jail and shoot Zach if he continued to hold out on them.

Macahan tried to talk him out of it, but Joshua wouldn't listen. And when Macahan blocked the batwing doors,

Joshua turned ugly and took a wild swing at him. Macahan easily blocked the punch, slammed his brother against the bar, and twisted his arm up behind his back. 'Pack it in, boy, or I'm going to have to cuff you.'

When Joshua continued to struggle, Macahan grabbed a pitcher of beer from the barkeep, and doused him with it. Sputtering and cursing, Joshua stopped resisting. Macahan released him, stood back and waited to see what his brother would do. Joshua remained dejectedly slumped over the bar. Suddenly, he burst into tears. It was more than Macahan could take. Throwing money on the bar for their drinks, he apologized to the barkeep for the ruckus and led his brother out.

★   ★   ★

They rode knee-to-knee back across the border and on through town without uttering a word. All around them townspeople and soldiers were pitching in to clean up the vandalism and destruction caused by the Villistas. The Commercial Hotel, the Lemmon & Romney Mercantile, and two small houses behind the hotel had burned to the ground. Glass shards from broken windows crunched underfoot. Bloodstains reddened the sandy streets where Mexicans and Americans had died. It had been a black day that would forever leave its historical imprint on the tiny hamlet of Columbus.

Once north of town, the brothers Macahan rode across the flat, scrub-covered desert toward the Florida Mountains. The sun burned through their shirts, toasting their backs. Tiny round-tailed horned lizards scattered ahead of them and, once, a disturbed rattler whirred its rattles threateningly at them before gliding off into the mesquite. And still they rode. Silent. Tight-lipped. Minds churning. Never looking at each other but always staring fixedly ahead.

They might have ridden all the way

to the mountains. But halfway there, rifle shots made them rein up and look behind them. It was Celia, waving as she galloped toward them on her dun. Whirling their mounts around, they rode back to meet her.

She was dressed like a vaquero and under her flat-crowned black hat, her hair was pulled back in a glistening black bun. Her flashing dark eyes were red-rimmed from crying, and she looked as only a mother can look when she has had her child torn from her. Macahan wished he could take her in his arms and make her pain disappear.

'Where have you been?' she said to Joshua. 'I've been half-crazed with worry.'

'Sorry.'

'Sorry?'

'Sorry.'

'After everything that has happened today you decide to disappear on me and all you can say is 'sorry'?'

'What do you want me to say?'

'I don't want you to say anything!'

'Then why are you screaming at me?'

'I'm not screaming,' she screamed. 'I just want you to know that if Mr. Ingalls hadn't seen you riding out this way, I'd still be looking for you!'

'I said I was sorry.'

'¡Madre de Dios, te voy a sacar el corazon!'

'Take it easy,' Macahan said.

'I'll tear your heart out, too,' she raged. 'You of all people, Ezra Macahan, you should know better.'

'It's not his fault,' Joshua said, 'It's mine. I went haywire when I heard they'd arrested Zach.'

Celia looked confused. 'Your brother? What're you talking about?'

'Let's all ride on back to the house,' Macahan said. 'I'll explain everything there.'

★   ★   ★

When he was all through explaining, Celia, who had listened in white-faced, fist-clenched silence, demanded that he wire the president and beg him to pardon Zachary so he could lead them to Daniel.

'Not that simple,' Macahan said. 'Any wire I'd send most likely wouldn't reach the president. Like I told Zach, I ain't that important.'

'Then find someone who is. Because if you don't, I swear to you on my father's grave I will hire men, gunmen or border trash if necessary, to break him out!'

'Take it easy.'

'Damn you, Ezra, *you* take it easy — '

'Celia, honey,' Josh began.

'Damn you, too,' she said. 'If you had been more of a man you would have defended our house against that pig!'

'That's not fair. I tried to — '

Macahan grabbed her roughly by the shoulders. 'How many men does he have to kill 'fore he gets to be a man in your eyes?'

Too incensed to find words, Celia slapped him.

Macahan's eyes watered. He turned and walked out.

'You had no call to do that,' Joshua said, and stormed after his brother.

Celia stood there, cheeks wet with tears, breasts heaving, trembling with a mixture of rage and something she had never felt before, a sense of fear and helplessness.

★ ★ ★

A few minutes later, calmer now, she found them standing beside the corral, elbows resting atop the fence, smoking in grim silence as they watched the golden dun pacing before them.

'*Me averguenzo de mi mismo,*' she said. '*¿Me puedes perdonas?*'

'Nothing to forgive,' Macahan said. 'Or to be ashamed of. I had no right to lay my hands on you.'

'You had every right. And you,' she said to Joshua, 'you have every right to hate me forever.'

'You know I'd never hate you, no

matter what you did.'

'I wish you would, *mi esposo*. It would help ease my shame.'

Joshua gently put his arms around her. 'Like Ezra said: there's nothing to feel ashamed about. What you said is true. I don't have any *cajones* — '

'I never said that.'

'I should have defended my family better. I don't know how, but I should've found a way . . . any way to protect you and Daniel. But I didn't. I didn't and that's something I'll always have to live — '

'Quit pounding on yourself,' Macahan said. 'It won't bring the boy back.'

'I know. The only way to do that is with Zach's help.'

'Fat chance of that.'

'I'm not talking about a pardon. That would take too long even if we could reach the president. But there's another way.' He turned to Celia. 'You gave me the idea.'

'*Yo? Cuando?*'

'A few minutes ago. When you said

you'd hire men to break Zach out. Well, you don't need to hire anyone. I'll do it myself.'

'Are you loco?' Macahan said. 'Or just anxious to get yourself smoked?'

'Neither,' Joshua said. 'I just want my son back.'

'Forget it.'

'You don't have to help.'

'I don't intend to.'

'Then why are you jawing at me?'

'Trying to set your brains straight.'

'You're wasting your time. Nothing you say is going to make me change my mind.'

'¡*Por el amor de Dios, paren!*' Celia said.

'Don't tell me to stop,' Joshua raged. 'Tell this mule-headed brother of mine! He's the one trying to stop me from getting Daniel back.'

'Stopping you from landing in the stockade's more like it,' Macahan said. He angrily wagged a finger in his brother's face. 'You so much as cast a shadow on that goddamn jail and I'll arrest you faster than you can spit.'

'Then you'll have to arrest me, because without Zach's help it could take forever to catch up with Acosta and, by then, Daniel could be . . . dead.'

He ground out his cigarette and hurried into the house.

Macahan looked at Celia, 'You got to stop him.

'*No puedo.*'

'Sure you can. You been ramrodding him ever since the day you two got hitched. So don't get coy on me now. Just haul yourself in there and make him see some sense.'

'Perhaps I don't want to.'

Macahan eyed her grimly. 'Don't mess with me, woman. You won't like the results.'

She met his glare without flinching. 'Don't threaten me, Ezra.'

'I'm not. I'm just asking you to stop my kid brother from sticking his head in a noose.'

Before she could answer, a cavalryman came galloping up. Reining his lathered mount in, he asked Celia where her husband was.

'Who wants to know?' Macahan said.

'The colonel, sir. He wants to see you both at headquarters. Right away!'

12

Behind his desk at company headquarters, Colonel Slocum looked sterner than usual. 'This is not easy for me to say,' he said when Macahan and Joshua stood before him. 'Especially in light of what I said during our last conversation.'

The brothers Macahan said nothing. Colonel Slocum smoothed his mustache and fiddled with papers on his desk. Then clearing his throat, he looked up and said: 'It concerns your brother, Lt. Zachary Macahan.'

'We know his name,' Macahan said. 'Now tell us what's wrong.'

'I'm afraid he's escaped.'

'W-What?' Joshua said. 'My God, when? How, sir?'

'While he was being escorted to the base.'

Macahan eyed the colonel suspiciously. 'You took him out of jail?'

'Yes.'

'Why, dammit?'

The colonel bristled. 'I don't like your tone, Marshal.'

'And I don't like what happened to my brother.'

'You accusing me of something?'

'Not if you tell me exactly how my brother managed to bust loose.'

'I don't have to tell you anything, Marshal. Least of all explain my actions. This was a military matter.'

'Or a cover-up.'

'Watch yourself, Macahan. You're on government property and I am the commanding officer. Marshal or no, inappropriate conduct will get you arrested.'

'That can work both ways, Colonel. You already got troubles of your own, do you want inherit more?'

'I beg your pardon — ?'

'There's folks in Washington already wondering how Pancho Villa and his boys managed to cross the border without you knowing and attack Columbus right under your nose. My guess is they're going to ask you some embarrassing questions. Do you really want the U.S. Marshal's office on your back as well?'

Colonel Slocum cleared his throat and smoothed his mustache. He was perfectly confident, he said, that he could answer any questions, official or otherwise, concerning the raid. Oh, there would be people who might accuse him of being asleep. Let them. He knew better. Without the use of spies or permission to cross the border, he had no choice but to wait for Villa to attack. When he did, the men of the 13th Cavalry performed brilliantly. Why, in just a few short hours they repulsed a surprise attack, even though outnumbered, and drove the enemy back into Mexico. And all with very few casualties of their own while inflicting heavy loss to the enemy.

'If everything's looking so damn rosy,' Macahan said, 'then why did you pull my brother out of jail?'

Colonel Slocum reddened. 'Again, I

don't like your tone. But if you must know, I ordered Lt. Macahan brought here for his own safety. One of my men heard rumors that people in town had discovered his identity and were calling for a rope.'

'That don't explain how he escaped.'

'Somehow the lieutenant got his hands on a pistol.'

''Somehow'? You tryin' to pin this on me, Colonel?'

'No, of course not, Marshal. Someone must have slipped it to him through the window. My aide checked, and the bars are just wide enough. Anyway, the lieutenant used it to disarm his escort, stole one of their horses and escaped.'

'Sir — '

'What is it, Corporal?'

'Was Zach shot escaping, sir?'

'Shots were fired at him, but to my knowledge Lt. Macahan was not hit.'

'Any idea where he went?' Macahan said.

'Last seen, he was fleeing to the border. Anything else?'

'Are you sending men after him, Colonel?'

'No. Every available man is needed here.' Colonel Slocum cleared his throat again and shuffled papers around before looking at Joshua. 'On another matter,' he said, his voice softening. 'I just found out, Corporal, that during the raid Villistas kidnapped your son.'

'Yes, sir. One of Villa's commanders, Manuel Acosta.'

'Scar?'

'Yes, sir.'

'You know that to be a fact?'

'Yes, sir, My wife, Celia, tried to stop him.'

'I see.' The colonel sighed, genuinely moved. 'I am deeply sorry, Corporal. I'm a father myself and I cannot begin to imagine how awful you must feel.'

'While you're all choked up,' Macahan said brutally, 'maybe you'd consider helping us get the boy back.'

'You know his whereabouts?'

'Not exactly. But if you'll recall, Colonel, I saw Scar with his men in

Janos, so I reckon that'd be a good starting point. If you could spare a scout and maybe a troop to help us comb the Sierra Madre — '

'That's absolutely out of the question, Marshal. Unless General Pershing receives orders from the president to cross the border, there will be no U.S. troops dispatched to Mexico.'

★ ★ ★

That night Macahan ate dinner with his brother and wife. Very little was said between them until the meal was almost over. Then Celia, who had eaten little, set her fork down, and quietly — almost too quietly — asked Joshua what he intended to do about rescuing their son.

'Ezra and I are riding down to Janos. From there, we'll start looking for Scar's stronghold. Won't be easy, now that Zach's run off, but — '

'Hang on,' Macahan said. 'I think Celia's got a plan.'

'Not a plan so much as an idea.'

'I'd like to hear it.'

'I will ride with you to Janos — '

'*You?*' Joshua said. 'No. Absolutely not. I won't let you.'

'Hold up, little brother. Let her talk.'

'I am Mexican,' Celia said. 'Villagers, children . . . *campesinos* in the fields . . . they will trust me and tell me things about Acosta they would not reveal to you.'

'Makes sense,' Macahan said.

'You finished?' Joshua said.

'My father was well-respected in Chihuahua. Many *hacendados* were his *compadres*. They trusted him and supported him against Huerta. Those who are still alive, have reason to hate Villa and Acosta. Both have raped their women and looted and burned their haciendas, killing many of their neighbors in the process. If one of them knows where *La Marcada Uno* is, they would like nothing better than to lead us to him.'

'Finished?' Joshua repeated.

119

'I promise I will not be a liability. I can ride as well as either of you, and my father taught me how to shoot.'

'Now, are you finished?'

'*Si, mi esposo.*'

'Then hear this: I don't care if you're Buffalo Bill and Annie Oakley combined and can track better than an Apache, you're not riding with us. And that's final.'

Celia, unfazed by his outburst, turned to Macahan. 'What do you think?'

'What do I think? I'll tell you what I think. *Dios nos ayude!*'

Celia smiled. 'It is God's help,' she said, 'that I am counting on most.'

13

The next morning, shortly after reveille, Macahan rode into Camp Furlong and presented his list of requirements to the quartermaster. The sergeant looked it over and saw Colonel Slocum's signature at the bottom. Though he was surprised that the military was supplying a civilian, albeit a U.S. deputy marshal with arms and provisions, it wasn't his place to argue with his commanding officer. He put up no resistance.

'I'll be able to issue you everything except hand grenades, Marshal.'

'Then I'll take dynamite.'

'We're fresh out of dynamite.'

'How about a machine gun?'

'Sorry. It ain't on the list.'

Macahan, who'd forged Colonel Slocum's signature, knew he was in no position to argue. He needed to be out of the camp and across the border before the C.O. came on duty.

'Reckon I'll have to make do,' he said. 'But I need this other stuff right away.'

The quartermaster chuckled. 'Don't you know nothing gets done right away in the army, Marshal? We operate on bureaucracy and red tape.'

'Ordinarily, that wouldn't bother me, Sarge. But like I told the colonel — a little boy's life is at stake. Every second I waste here could be a second closer to him dying.'

'Little boy — *what* little boy?'

Macahan quickly explained about the kidnapping of his brother's son.

The quartermaster knew and liked Joshua, and his whole demeanor changed. 'Tell you what, Marshal — you go pick up your ammo and the mule at the stables. By the time you get back, everything will be ready.'

'Good man.' Macahan hurried off.

When he returned shortly, the quartermaster not only had the supplies ready but he also had two soldiers standing by, ready to help Macahan load everything onto the pack mule. They ticked off the list together. The quartermaster had only changed one item: 'I gave you a five-gallon can of water instead of extra canteens. Never know about that Chihuahuan desert. I seen water holes down there dry up quicker than you can blink. Reckon it's better to be safe than sorry, eh?'

Mahacan nodded. Much as he appreciated the sergeant's help, valuable minutes were ticking away and any second he expected to see Colonel Slocum entering camp. 'Well, I better be making dust,' he said. 'Thanks for everything, Sarge.'

'My pleasure, Marshal. And I'm sorry about the machine gun. But in a way you're better off. Them dumb Ben-As jam so much you're taking your goddamn life in your hands every time you use one.'

'I saw that firsthand during the raid,' Macahan said. ''Bout time Uncle Sam switched to another weapon.' Shaking the quartermaster's hand, he mounted up and led the heavily loaded mule out of camp and onto the road leading to the border.

About two miles south of camp, Joshua and Celia were waiting with their horses beside Quail Rocks. They rose to greet him.

'I've got to hand it to you,' Joshua told his brother. 'I never thought it would work.'

'Perhaps you should consider changing vocations,' Celia laughed. 'There's more money in forging than wearing a tin star.'

'Tin stars don't land you in the hoosegow,' said Macahan. 'And I've seen enough jails to last me ten lifetimes.'

Joshua, who had been looking north along the Deming Road, pulled his campaign hat firmly down on his head. 'If you don't want to see any more,' he said. 'I recommend we head for the border *muy pronto*.' He pointed to something in the distance, something that was coming very fast and kicking up a lot of dust.

'What is that?' said Celia.

'Colonel Slocum's new motorwagon.'

'Motorwagon?'

'It's some kind of new-fangled machine on wheels. The Army's hoping one day it'll replace the horse.'

'Damn,' Macahan said. 'I sure hope this mule's got some giddyup in him.'

BOOK TWO

BOOK TWO

14

They had ridden through some rocky hill country under a spanking sun and were now crossing unbroken wasteland, the border some forty-odd miles behind them. It was even hotter on the flatland. Macahan, who had known Texas heat all his life, felt as if the sun was boiling his brains.

Ahead lay the Guzman Basin. They could see the sunlight glittering on the ruffled waters of *Laguna de Guzman*. To the west, across the ever-winding *Rio Casas Grandes* and beyond the foothills, loomed the towering peaks of the Sierra Madre Occidental. A cool wind off the lake made the intense heat a little more bearable, but buffeted a flock of migrating white cranes flying overhead.

No one had spoken for what seemed like hours. Now, as the wind died and the heat engulfed them again, Celia lowered the bandanna covering her mouth and nose and asked Macahan how much farther.

'Half hour, most.'

'You need a rest?' Joshua asked his wife.

'Do you need a rest?'

'No.'

'Then why should I?'

'I . . . I don't know.'

'Then do not assume what I need.'

Stung, Joshua shot her an angry look. 'Why must you turn everything I say into a competition?'

'Why must you treat me like a two-year-old?'

'Now, now, you two,' Macahan chided. 'Play nice.'

'*Perdoname*,' Celia said. '*Es el calor. Creo que es asfixiante.*' Pulling her bandanna back over her nose, she rode on in silence.

'She's right,' Joshua said. 'This damn heat *is* suffocating. Every time I take a breath feels like my lungs are on fire.'

Knowing that the farther south they rode, the worse it would be, Macahan didn't say anything. Already he was beginning to regret bringing Celia along. And for a bigger reason than her independence and fiery temper.

A small bright red bird slanted past their faces. Wings fanning, it settled on a clump of mesquite and cocked its head at them. It caught Macahan's eye and without thinking he said: 'Vermillion flycatcher.'

Joshua looked surprised. 'I didn't know you knew anything about birds.'

'I don't.'

'Then how'd you know what that one was?'

'I . . . uh . . . ' Trapped, Macahan said: 'I sort of do and I don't.'

'Sounds like you're embarrassed to talk about it.'

'Why should I be embarrassed?'

'You tell *me*.'

'Well, I ain't.'

Joshua looked at Celia. 'Does he seem embarrassed to you?'

'Like a man caught with his pants down.'

'Aw, hell,' said Macahan. 'Reckon I can tell you. About a year ago I came upon this book. It had been left behind in a hotel room. Had all these colored bird drawings in it — done by some famous fella from back east. Don't recall his name but — '

'Audubon?' Celia said.

'Sounds about right. They were the most detailed drawings of birds you ever saw. Almost flew off the pages at you. Some I'd seen, some I hadn't. I wasn't sleeping so good at the time so I read it, cover to cover. Was sunup 'fore I knew it. Got me to thinking. Up till then I'd been wondering what I'd do if I ever retired and — '

'You're going to take up ornithology?' Celia said.

'I'm goin' to draw birds, if that's what you mean.'

'Miracles never cease,' Joshua said.

They skirted the edge of the giant basin and rode up a steep rise and entered a narrow rocky canyon cut out of the foothills. A stand of bleached cottonwoods grew alongside a tiny creek. The trees all but hid a log-and-adobe shack and a small plank barn built against the rocks.

As they rode closer, their horses snorted and became nervous. The Army pack mule stopped, brayed fearfully, and jerked on its rope almost unseating Macahan, who was holding it.

'What's going on?' Joshua said.

'Must've smelled something they don't like. 'Here,' he handed the rope to Joshua and kneed his horse toward the shack. Normally obedient, the bay fought him and shied when urged forward.

Cursing it, Macahan dismounted, tied the reins to a tree, and walked the rest of the way. Between the trees he could see the door of the shack was open. A red roan mustang watched him from a log-corral beside the barn. No one was around. He continued walking, hands swinging loosely at his sides, ready to slap leather if necessary.

He passed between two large flat rocks. There was sound above him fainter than a whisper. Macahan looked up but he was too late. Two wolves leaped down in front of him. They landed without sound, quieter than ghosts, and faced him less than a step away. Ears flattened, fur bristling along their back, they snarled at him but did not attack. They were young males; brothers. Both weighed about ninety pounds, had dense rust-colored fur with light gray underparts and blazing yellow eyes.

All Macahan saw was their fangs. He stopped and felt his skin crawl. 'Lincoln,' he said, keeping his voice steady. 'Linc, it's me, Macahan. Can you hear me?'

For a moment the only sound was the low snarling of the wolves.

Then someone said: 'I hear you, Macahan.'

'Call off your dogs.'

An Apache stepped silently from

behind the rocks. He did not look like much. Short and wiry as ocotillo, he was pushing forty and had a slight paunch. His bronze leathery face was broad and flat, like his nose, and his almond-shaped black eyes and high cheekbones made him look Mongolian. He was unarmed save for a large, curved, horn-handled knife sheathed at his side. He wore a brown vest over his long-sleeve blue shirt and an old khaki hat from under which hung lank black hair. His sun-faded U.S. cavalry pants were tucked into knee-high moccasins and hanging between his legs was a white cotton breechcloth. He seemed amused by Macahan's alarm.

'They're wolves, not dogs, Macahan. Lobos.'

'I know what the hell they are. Judas, I know a goddamn wolf when I see one.'

'Is that why you're about to soil your bloody britches?'

'Very funny.'

'I make a joke, Macahan.'

135

'An Apache with a phony British accent. It's a goddamn joke all right.'

'No need to throw a fit. Even famous lawmen are permitted to be afraid of lobos.'

'I ain't afraid, you damn Injun. I just got a healthy respect for anything that can eat me.'

'If you knew anything about wolves you'd know they only eat when they are hungry.'

'You know that. I know that. But do *they* know that?'

'That is an old tired cavalry joke, Macahan.'

'Well forgive me but right now I feel old and tired. Now if you want me to shoot 'em, I will.'

'Be interesting to watch you try. They can grab a rattler in mid-strike. Can you do that, Macahan?'

'Most likely not. But I sure as hell can shoot you, *amigo*, so maybe it's time you quit funnin' me and called off your pets.'

The Apache didn't move or say

anything but in some way he communicated with the wolves because suddenly they stopped snarling. Stiff-legged and on their toes, they walked slowly around Macahan, sniffing at his jeans and boots. He did not move. He scarcely breathed. One of the wolves stopped beside him and leaned against his leg. He felt its heart beating. Or was it his own? Meanwhile, the other wolf urinated on his boot.

Macahan wanted to kick it but decided that might be a mistake. He looked at Lincoln standing stoically before him. 'Do you reckon they know my scent by now?'

Suddenly the wolves leaped high in the air, backs arched, tails thrust out, as if on springs. Momentarily they seemed to be floating. Then they landed, cat-like, on all four paws and ran off, playfully jostling each other.

'Good,' the Apache said. 'They have accepted you.'

'Can't tell you how excited that makes me,' Macahan said. Turning, he signaled to Celia and his brother to come ahead.

⋆   ⋆   ⋆

With sunset less than an hour away, Macahan suggested they make camp in the canyon. The Apache became offended and insisted they put their horses and mule in the barn and all sleep in his shack. Though only one room and totally without furniture and windows, it was weather-proof and had an old iron stove, a chimney, and plenty of straw on the dirt floor.

Celia, for one, was delighted. She had already spent two nights on the trail and looked forward to sleeping under a roof. She was also fascinated by Lincoln. Educated at Carlisle, he was literate and spoke three languages fluently: Apache, Spanish, and English. He could also mimic a British accent, having spent time guiding a pompous English nobleman who was obsessed with shooting trophy heads — elk, antelope, mountain lion, and deer. The pay was excellent; far more than an Indian could earn scouting for the Army. But killing for sport did not sit well with Lincoln, especially when so many of his people were starving on reservations, and after a few weeks he resigned and went back to scout for General Crooke who was waging war against the Apaches. Fighting his own people was dangerous work and when the war ended in '86 with Geronimo's capture, Lincoln considered himself fortunate to be alive. He also considered himself fortunate not to be one of the many Apache scouts whose loyalty and bravery Washington rewarded by arresting and imprisoning them in Florida with Geronimo and his followers. Instead, Lincoln was decorated for valor and received his medal at the White House from President Stephen Grover Cleveland.

Celia tried to get him to describe his war experiences, but he was too modest to go into detail and finally she gave up and asked him how he'd ended up with two wolves as pets. They weren't pets, he said. They just happened to live in the same *barranca* together. They led their lives; he led his. But surely he fed them, didn't he? Looked after them? No, Lincoln said. He didn't feed them or look after them or interfere in anything they did. In fact, he added, if anything, they looked after *him*. Occasionally he'd hear them hunting at night and in the morning he'd find a dead rabbit or fox or a migrating goose dead outside his door. At first he'd thought it was an accident; that maybe a bear had surprised them, causing them to drop their prey in order to escape. But after it happened a few more times, he realized it was some kind of tribute, as if the wolves wanted him to understand they appreciated being left alone.

That night they all sat around a fire on the dirt floor of the shack and stuffed themselves full of rabbit stew and corn spiced with jalapenos and afterward drank mescal from an earthen jug that Lincoln passed around. The mescal was potent. It made their heads swim and temporarily lifted their spirits, allowing them to forget about Daniel's kidnapping for a while. But it also made them a little drunk and they finished the bowl wishing there was more.

Later, while Celia and Lincoln were talking, Joshua asked Macahan to join him outside for a smoke. Sensing his brother had something on his mind, Macahan agreed. It was crisp, clear, and desert-cold outside. They leaned against a rock under an inky sky aglitter with stars, smoking and listening to the two wolves howling at the moon on the rim of the canyon.

'So what's on your mind?' Macahan said.

'On my mind?'

'Yeah, what'd you want to tell me?'

'Nothing.'

'Nothing?'

Joshua looked away as if he'd changed his mind.

'You better hadn't drug these old bones away from the fire for nothing.'

'You're not old. You're not even fifty.'

'Old enough to know when something's gnawing on my kid brother.'

'You won't get sore if I tell you?'

'I'll get sore if you don't.'

'It's Lincoln.'

'What about him?'

'Back in Columbus, when you said you were going to ask him to join us I thought . . . I mean, I expected . . .'

'What?'

'Well, you know . . .'

'Tell me, dammit.'

'More.'

'More?'

Joshua shrugged lamely. 'Well, you did make him sound special.'

'He is special. Maybe the most special fighting man you'll ever meet.'

'Sure doesn't look it.'

'He don't have to.'

'What do you mean?'

'He's already proved it. That's good enough for him.'

142

'Dammit, what's so special about him?'

'You'll find out when we reach Scar's stronghold.'

'Tell me now. I got a right to know, haven't I?'

'I reckon.' Macahan blew a smoke ring toward the stars. 'Before Lincoln became a Christian his tribal name was He Who Walks Without Sound. Even in dry brush you can't hear him coming. He can see in the dark and get within a whisker of you without you ever knowing. When he was scouting for General Crooke, he put the fear of God into the Broncos. Used to go into their camps at night and cut their throats while they were sleeping. Terrified them, because they believed their spirits would get lost in the dark. When it comes time, and if he agrees to hook up with us, I'll send him into Acosta's stronghold. He'll count heads so we'll know how many men we're up against, pinpoint where the lookouts are posted, and, most important, find out where

Scar's keeping Daniel. That special enough for you?'

'I'm sorry,' Joshua said. 'I shouldn't have doubted you.'

'Doubt me all you want. But don't doubt that Injun inside. He may not look special, but he's got something special hanging around his neck that tells you more about him than I ever could in a month of Mondays.'

'What is it?'

'Ask him to show it to you sometime. Reckon then you'll know what I mean.' Macahan ground out his cigarette beneath his heel. 'Now let's bed down. We got hard riding ahead of us tomorrow.'

* * *

Macahan woke in the middle of the night. He realized the mescal must have been stronger than he thought because the red roan mustang stood looking at him from across the room. He blinked, expecting it to disappear. When it did not he sat up and nudged the Apache curled under a blanket beside him.

'What the hell?' he whispered.

'There was no room for him in the barn,' Lincoln said.

'What's wrong with the corral?'

'Lobos.'

'Lobos?'

'They would eat him if I left him out.'

'I thought you and them wolves lived in harmony.'

'They still have to eat.'

'You could always shoot 'em.'

'They were here first.'

Macahan heard a steady swishing sound. The roan was urinating on the straw under its hooves.

'You're the one I should shoot,' he growled.

'You get used to it,' Lincoln said. He rolled onto his side away from Macahan, who lay back and covered his face with his blanket.

Several minutes passed. The roan grunted and flopped down on the straw.

Its breathing was louder than Joshua's snoring.

'Tomorrow, Macahan, you will be riding on to Janos?'

'Yep.'

'I'm glad. I don't wish to offend an old friend.'

Macahan chuckled. He admired this humble, dry-humored Apache above all others. He was the only man he truly felt comfortable around.

'If you felt like tagging along I wouldn't stop you.'

'You inviting me?'

'Hell, no.'

'But you won't stop me if I tag along?'

'Reckon not.'

'Sure sounds like an invitation to me.'

'Well, it ain't. So get that out of your mind.'

'You just won't stop me if I tag along?'

'Correct.'

'Then I will ride with you.'

'Maybe you should hear what you're getting into first.'

'What would that change?'

'Maybe your mind.'

'Macahan, I live with wolves and sleep with a horse that pisses on my floor. How much bleaker can my future get?'

15

So now there were four of them. At sunup, after breakfasting on coffee, cold rabbit and tortillas left over from the night before, they mounted up and rode out of the canyon. A dense mist blanketed the ground. It hid the two wolves that came running out of the cottonwoods and loped after the riders.

With Macahan leading, they descended to the desert floor. Here, a bitter wind off the lake cut into them and whipped the horses' manes. They pulled their coat collars up. Everyone was shivering except the Apache. He seemed impervious to the weather. As they skirted some rocks and headed southwest, Macahan suddenly noticed the wolves loping along behind them.

'We got company.'

'They won't bother us,' the Apache said.

'They're already bothering me. Tell them to go home.'

'They're not pets. They go where they go.'

'Then I reckon it's up to me to send 'em some place else.' Macahan reached for his Winchester.

'Oh, let them be, Ezra,' Celia said. 'They're not harming anyone.'

'They hamstring our mule and we have to carry the packs, I'll be reminding you about that.'

The sun came up over their shoulders. It gradually burned off the ground mist and, as the day wore on, hammered down on them. On all sides the arid sun-baked desert was dominated by creosote bushes, mesquite, yucca, and scattered rocks. Dry river-beds and ravines appeared out of nowhere. It was a great place for an ambush, and Macahan was glad the Apaches were now on reservations and that the local *bandidos* seldom left the safety of the mountains.

They rode on. The terrain was

monotonous. Combined with the heat, it made them drowsy. The three men for different reasons were accustomed to long hours in the saddle; but Celia was not. She dozed off. Her mount responded by slowing down. Almost imperceptibly, Celia began to slip from her saddle. Fortunately, Macahan had noticed she was growing drowsy and dropped back to ride with her. He grabbed her before she lost her stirrups. Startled, she woke just as he was propping her up. She smiled and thanked him with her eyes. He smiled back. At the same time, he silently chided himself for the feelings he had for her. The life of his nephew was in jeopardy and all he should have been thinking about was rescuing Daniel. Celia seemed to sense how he felt and pressed her gloved hand fondly over his. Thank you, she mouthed at him.

Macahan nodded; then troubled by his improper thoughts, he kicked his horse into a canter and rode alongside the Apache. Lincoln never turned around and, unless he had eyes in the back of his head, he could not have seen what happened between Macahan and Celia. Yet Macahan knew that nothing ever went unnoticed by him. He was right. Lapsing into his fake, cultured British accent, Lincoln spoke without looking at his longtime friend.

'I say, old chap, by any chance have you ever read Thomas Malory's *Le Morte d'Arthur*?'

'Nope,' Macahan said. 'And I ain't caught the clap neither.'

'You should, dear boy.'

'Catch the clap?'

'Read the book.'

'Why? What's it about?'

'Many things . . . knighthood, honor, chivalry . . . but most of all, it's about love and betrayal.'

Macahan ignored the dig. 'Reckon I'll stick to my birds,' he said.

Throats parched, they drank warm metallic-tasting water from their canteens and tried to cool off by wetting their bandannas before knotting them around their necks. Mid-morning they stopped in the shade of some rocks to rest and water the horses and the mule from their cupped hands. The wolves ran their tongues out as if laughing at them and took off into the desert.

'Will they come back?' Celia said.

Lincoln shrugged. 'They go where they go, señora.'

'I hope they do. I'm just getting used to them.'

Stretched out on the warm sand the four of them ate handfuls of dry corn, jerky and tortillas wrapped around beans and rice. Attracted by the smell of food, a coyote suddenly appeared from a gully and eyed them curiously. Celia threw it a piece of jerky. The coyote skittered away a few yards then cautiously returned, sniffed at the meat, and gobbled it down. It stood there another moment, watchful, waiting, ready to flee, yet hungry enough that when Celia did not throw it any more food, it yapped at her.

'See what you've started,' Macahan

grumbled. 'Now we'll have a damn coyote tagging along as well as them wolves.'

'All we need is his mate,' Joshua said, laughing, 'and then we'll be like Noah's Ark.'

Just then one of the wolves struck. It leaped from a nearby rock and knocked the surprised coyote sprawling. It instantly regained its feet and easily avoided the wolf's next lunge.

'Run, little coyote,' said Celia.

The coyote obeyed her. It was quicker than the wolf in a short sprint and would have escaped. But it had not traveled more than twenty yards when the other wolf sprang from behind a clump of mesquite. It grabbed the coyote by the throat and dragged it down. The first wolf raced up and grabbed a hind leg, breaking it in one bite. The coyote struggled mightily. But the first wolf clamped its jaws, crushing the coyote's jugular, ending it.

Celia looked away. '*Dios Mio*, I feel awful,' she said, 'If I hadn't fed it, it would have gone on its way and still be alive.'

'But the wolves would be hungry,' Lincoln said.

'Survival of the fittest,' Macahan said.

'I know that,' Celia said. 'But I still wish I hadn't fed it.'

They rode for another two hours, passing a small pewter-colored lake and twice fording the snakelike *Rio Casas Grandes*. They also skirted several tiny villages in case Acosta had spies there. By now the wolves had caught up with them. Their jaws and ruff were matted with dried blood. They loped along, tirelessly, never gaining or losing ground.

By late afternoon they had reached the yellow grassy plain that sloped southward down to Janos. It was still hot but the landscape had changed. There was more water and with water came greenery and wild life. Rabbits hopped ahead of them, ground squirrels watched them from their holes and, overhead, hawks drifted lazily on rising thermals.

Macahan reined up by a shallow tree-lined creek fed by the Janos River. It looked familiar and he remembered it was the same stream he had used to hide the blood dripping from the blanket-wrapped outlaws he'd killed the last time he was here. It was only a week or so ago but it felt like a lifetime. No, he thought. Not quite a lifetime. A lifetime was how long it felt when he thought about Prudence and how much he had loved her and what great times they had had together and how he'd never stopped aching for her. Dammit, there you go again, he thought angrily. Reminiscing!

His thoughts were interrupted by something bumping against his leg. It was the knee of the Apache who had ridden alongside him. Macahan looked questioningly at him. '*¿nt'e nant'ii?*'

'I don't want anything.'

'Then why do I feel a lecture comin' on?'

'Advice is not a lecture.'

'It's worse.'

'How do you know until you hear it?'

''Cause your advice always stinks.'

'Yet you've taken it on several occasions.'

'And always regretted it later. Oh all right,' Macahan said as the Apache looked hurt. 'I'll bite. What's your goddamn advice?'

'It's time you took a woman, Macahan.'

'Jees-us.' Macahan rolled his eyes. 'Coming from you, *amigo*, that's a joke. Hell, a hermit crab has had more women than you.'

'At least I am not talking to myself.'

'I wasn't talking to myself. I was thinking aloud.'

'If you'd married Prudence you wouldn't need to think aloud, either.'

'For a lousy cigar store Injun,' Macahan said, 'you got a smart mouth.'

'Education evil thing,' Lincoln said woodenly. 'Make Indian think him equal.'

'Since when'd you start talking pidgin English?'

'Since you poked fun at my British accent.'

'I didn't poke fun at it. I said you were a joke.'

'Same thing.'

'Well, while you're sulking, *amigo*, how about doing something useful for a change?'

'Like ride into Janos ahead of you and see if any of Scar's men are in town?'

'You're readin' my mind.'

'And while this 'sulking Injun' is risking his neck scouting around for you, what will *Señor Blanco* be doing?'

'Taking a nap, most likely. All this palavering has damn near wore me out.'

Chuckling, the Apache spun his mustang around and rode off.

Macahan dismounted, turned his horse loose to drink, and tended to the pack mule. Downstream, Joshua was watering his horse. Nearer to Macahan, Celia had already watered hers and now stood wiping her face with her wet bandanna. She watched the Apache riding off across the plain, trailed by the two wolves.

'We're lucky to have him, aren't we?'

'Very lucky,' Macahan said. 'Linc's like a one-man army.'

'Strange how those wolves follow him around like dogs.'

'Difference is dogs don't eat you when they're hungry.'

Celia laughed. 'Macahan,' she said. 'You should do more of that.'

'When we get Daniel back, I will.'

'I'll hold you to that.'

'Does that mean you'll come around more often?'

'Means I'll try.'

She looked up into his rugged, leathery face. 'Macahan,' she said.

He saw his miniature reflection in her dark eyes and it seemed to be mocking him. He stepped back and caught Joshua watching him. He had nothing to feel guilty about yet he did, and it bothered him.

'We should get some rest,' he said gruffly. Tying the mule's reins to a tree, he sat in the shade with his back to a cottonwood, pulled his hat over his face, and dozed off.

Joshua joined Celia under the trees. Lying on his side with his head propped up by one hand, he studied her. She lay on her back, hands folded behind her head, looking up through the leafy ceiling at the nude blue sky. The joy of knowing she was his wife made his heart pound.

'I'm sorry you think I treat you like a child,' he said.

'You don't. That was the heat talking.'

'It's just that I love you so damn much and don't want anything to happen to you.'

'I feel the same about you.'

'You mean that?'

'Would I say it if I didn't?'

'I hope not.'

'Well, I wouldn't.'

'No, of course not.'

159

'It's just lately . . . everything seems to have gone wrong,'

'It has been piling up,' he admitted.

'We've been so lucky up to now.'

'We'll be lucky again.'

'Now we seem to have no luck at all.'

'We'll be lucky again; don't worry.'

'*No suerte en esta situacion*,' she repeated.

Joshua didn't know what to say.

'For the first time in my life, Josh, I'm frightened.'

'Don't be. We'll get Daniel back, I promise.'

'I know. But what if we don't?'

'We will.'

'I know. But what if we don't? What if we really don't?'

'We will, I tell you. Got my word on it.'

She smiled, tight-lipped. 'Now you sound like Ezra.'

He didn't want to sound like his brother; he wanted to sound like himself.

'I mean it,' he said. He sat up to

emphasize his words. 'I'll do whatever it takes, I swear. And you know Ezra and Lincoln will, too.' He waited for her to respond. When she remained silent, he turned and looked at her. She had copied Macahan: covered her face with her flat-brimmed black gaucho hat and appeared to be asleep.

Joshua wanted to hold her in his arms. But he knew she needed rest more than his affection. Feeling rejected, he leaned back against the tree and closed his eyes. But it was worse with his eyes closed. Opening them, he looked beyond the tall green grass at the shallow, fast-moving stream. It was coming from somewhere and going somewhere. It had purpose and it belonged.

He had no purpose and felt like he didn't belong anywhere. In fact, he'd never felt so alone and lonely in his whole life.

16

Macahan stood, Winchester in hand, angrily watching the two riders crossing the grassy plain toward him. Behind them, with the sun having sunk lower on the horizon, he could just make out the outskirts of Janos.

I should have knowed it, he thought. Dammit to hell, I should have knowed it all along. And if I hadn't had my mind between my legs, I would have. I'm too smart not to.

The riders came closer. One rode a red roan mustang; the other a finely bred, long-legged Andulusian stallion as gold as a double eagle. Well, thought Macahan, he ain't lost his taste in horseflesh, that's for sure.

When the riders were still fifty yards off, the Apache continued riding but the other rider reined up and waited, watching to see how Macahan reacted.

'He wants to know if he's welcome,' Lincoln said, dismounting.

'He ain't,' Macahan said. 'And the son of a bitch knows he ain't. But he also knows how much we need him. So go get him.'

'He won't come. Not till you wave him in.'

'I'll wave him in. I'll wave him in and stretch his goddamn neck from one of those cottonwoods.'

'That's what he's worried about.'

Macahan expelled his anger in an explosive sigh. Then, resigned, he signaled for the rider to approach. 'Go wake up Josh,' he said. 'He ought to be here. By the way,' he added as Lincoln moved off. 'Did you see any of Acosta's men in the village?'

'No.'

'How about anything else I should fret about?'

The Apache grinned. 'Just a squaw with a papoose in the oven.'

* * *

The brothers Macahan had moved off to one side to talk, leaving Celia alone with Lincoln.

'I want it straight,' Macahan told Zachary. 'No more goddamn lies, you understand?'

'I didn't lie to you,' Zachary said. 'I just didn't tell you everything.'

'Why not?' Joshua said. 'We're your brothers. We had a right to know what you were going to do.'

'And if I'd told you, what would you have done? You,' he said to Macahan, 'would have lectured me, given me a millions reasons why I shouldn't try to escape and you, Josh, you would've tried to help me and I didn't want that. I didn't want either of you involved. That way if anything went sour — '

Macahan cut him off. 'Even if you're tellin' the truth — which I doubt — that still don't excuse you for making us think you knew where Scar had taken Daniel.'

'But it's true,' Zachary said. 'I *do* know where.'

'You do?' Joshua said.

'Yes. 'Least, I know where his stronghold is. And I'd bet a dollar to a peso that that's where he's stashed Daniel.'

'And you'll take us there?'

'Why do you think I was in Janos, waiting for you to show up?'

'Hiding out?' Macahan said.

'In Janos? Garden spot of Chihuahua? Christ, give me some credit. Believe me, I know a hundred better places to hide.'

He seemed to be telling the truth, but Macahan couldn't be sure. 'How'd you know we were coming to Janos?'

'You told me, when we were talking in jail. Remember?'

Macahan didn't remember. He thought back to their conversation. He was positive he hadn't mentioned Janos. But if that was true, how did Zachary know? Certainly neither Josh nor Celia could have told him. So, who did? Then it hit him. Colonel Herbert J. Slocum. He had told the colonel about seeing Scar and his men at Janos, and then later, after Daniel's kidnapping, mentioned it again, calling it a 'good starting point' to begin looking for Scar's stronghold. Hell, it all tied together. He had never quite swallowed the colonel's story about how Zachary had escaped and now he was more convinced than ever that Slocum had made it up to cover the truth. What the truth was exactly, and why a long-time stalwart cavalry officer would risk his career to lie for his brother — a deserter! — Macahan didn't know. But, when it was time, he intended to find out.

'I reckon you're telling the truth,' he said grudgingly.

'Then all's forgiven?'

Macahan hesitated, looked at Joshua who eagerly nodded, and then extended his hand to Zachary. 'Why not? Don't do no good holding a grudge. 'Specially now when we need each other. You help us get Daniel and I'll be beholding to you for the rest of my natural.'

That night they camped in a remote little canyon in the hills. They hobbled the horses and the pack mule so they couldn't wander off and be attacked by the wolves; then, confident they could not be seen, built a fire over which Lincoln cooked a bean, onion, corn, chili, rattlesnake stew that no one could deny was tasty.

Since Zachary's arrival, everyone's mood had brightened. He had assured them that Scar's stronghold wasn't more than a day's ride away. He had also heard rumors in the village that since the Columbus raid, which even the staunchest Villistas admitted was a defeat, many of the men had returned to their farms, lessening the number guarding the stronghold. On top of that, he broke out a bottle of brandy he had bought from a gambler in Casas Grandes and, for the moment at least, everything seemed a lot rosier.

After the meal, while they were

passing the bottle around, he showed them a map he had drawn that showed how to reach the stronghold. That way he said, if anything happened to him prior to them getting there, they would still be able to find it and hopefully rescue Daniel.

'Nothing's going to happen,' Joshua said. 'It can't. Not now we're this close to getting him back.'

'I'll drink to that,' Zachary said. 'Hand me that bottle, *hermano*.' He looked off into the darkness. 'I need to get drunk anyway so I can go to sleep without worrying about getting eaten by those damned wolves.'

Everyone laughed. Everyone but the Apache.

'What if Daniel isn't there?' he said.

There was a silence as everyone exchanged uneasy looks.

'Don't say that,' Joshua said angrily. 'He's got to be there.'

'No, no, Linc's right,' Macahan said. 'It's possible he isn't. Acosta could be holding him closer to the border so he

can turn him over once he's paid off.'
He turned to Zachary. 'You know Scar
better than any of us. If he ain't holding
Daniel at his stronghold, where else
would he take him?'

'I've no idea.'

'What makes you so sure Scar is at
his stronghold?' Celia said.

'The man is a creature of habit. After
every raid or sortie with Villa, he's
always gone back there.'

'And it's heavily guarded?'

'Lookouts everywhere. Machine guns
guarding the entrance. A water tower
made out of iron. A restored hacienda
with extra thick walls and a double-tile
roof. My God, the place is a veritable
fortress.'

'Okay,' Macahan said. 'I reckon we'll
go on your say-so.'

'Only one thing bothers me,' Zachary
said. 'Why didn't Scar demand any
ransom? Most kidnappers want their
money fast. Acosta's no exception. I
would've thought one of his henchmen
would have been slipping notes under

Josh's door ten minutes after the kidnapping.'

'That's been chewin' on me, too,' Macahan said. 'Only thing I can think of is Scar heard the rumors about the president maybe sending Black Jack Pershing and an army into Mexico to capture Villa, and decided to hole up until things cooled down. I'm not saying I'm right, but it would explain why Acosta hasn't made any ransom demands.'

There was silence as the others mulled over his words. In the hills not too far away, the wolves began howling.

'By God, I hate that sound,' Macahan said. 'Sends shivers up my spine.'

'Makes me feel like Satan walked over my grave,' Joshua said.

'Forget the wolves,' said Zachary. 'I've got an idea how we can find out if Daniel is at the stronghold without risking anyone's neck.'

'We're listening,' Macahan said.

'There's a woman in Janos — Consuelo. She is a favorite of Scar's men.'

'A whore, you mean?' said Joshua.

'*Si, hermano*. And from what I hear, a very mercenary one.'

'Go on.'

'She has eyes and ears everywhere.'

'And you figure she might've heard one of Scar's men talking about a gringo kid for ransom, that it?' said Macahan.

'Exactly. Of course she'll expect to be paid for her trouble.'

'We will pay her anything she asks,' Celia said.

'There's your answer,' Macahan said to Zachary.

'What if she plays us for fools?' Lincoln said. 'Takes the money and betrays us to Scar?'

'Don't you ever get tired of being so optimistic?' Joshua said.

'Forget the sarcasm,' Macahan said. 'Linc's just playing Devil's Advocate. Be grateful he is. We got more than ourselves to worry about. We got to decide what's best for Daniel.'

'I think it's worth the risk,' Celia said.

'I agree,' Joshua said. 'How else are we going to know if he's being held in the stronghold?

'I will find a way to get into the hacienda and tell you myself,' said the Apache.

'And if he isn't,' Zachary said, 'you've not only risked your life for nothing but we've wasted a lot of valuable time. My way's not only safe, it's quick.'

Macahan looked at Joshua and Celia and saw they were behind Zachary's idea. 'Okay, it's settled then. Now, question is: who's going to talk to her?'

'Me,' said Zachary. 'I know Consuelo, and she's very receptive to me.'

'Fair enough,' Macahan said. 'Tomorrow you ride in early and see what you can worm out of her.'

'Consider it done, *hermano*.'

* * *

That night they kept piling mesquite on the fire to keep it burning. By its light, they pored over the map and formed a plan of attack. Scar's stronghold was in a steep-walled canyon with a narrow entrance that Zachary said was guarded day and night. When Macahan asked if it was the only entry, Zachary replied that it was the only one that was accessible. The other end of the canyon, where Acosta's hacienda stood, was blocked by a mountain of massive, slab-like volcanic rocks known as *La Escalera del Diablo*. The rocks could be scaled from the canyon side if absolutely necessary — in other words if Scar and his men were forced to escape — but it was inaccessible from the outside; so inaccessible in fact, Acosta didn't even bother to post lookouts. 'And before you say that everything can be climbed,' Zachary said to Macahan, 'let me assure that the Devil's Stairway can't. I've seen it, and I know. Not even you,' he added to the Apache, 'could make it. And God knows you're half goat.'

Macahan smoked thoughtfully for a moment. 'We must find a way to make

Scar think that's where the attack's coming from.'

'A diversion?' Joshua said.

Macahan nodded. 'Too bad we don't have any dynamite. We could tie the sticks to arrows and Geronimo here could shoot 'em over the top. With short fuses they'd explode just as they hit the target and make it seem like a whole army was attacking.'

'Dynamite may not be out of the question,' Zachary said.

'You know where some is?'

'More than we need. But — '

'Why does there always have to be a 'but'?' Celia said.

''Cause the Good Lord wants to make sure life ain't easy,' Macahan said. He turned back to Zachary. 'Where is it? In Scar's stronghold?'

'In the cellar of his hacienda.'

'Figures.'

'Son of a bitch has been stock-piling it ever since the revolution went south on Villa. Told me that with enough of it, and with the machine guns he's got

174

covering the entrance, he can fight off the Carrancitas forever.'

There was silence as the consequences of what lay ahead for them sank deeper into their minds.

'Well,' Macahan said finally, 'we'd better quit this powwow and bed down. You especially,' he needled the Apache. 'You're going to need all your strength when you sneak in and grab the dynamite.'

Lincoln never even blinked.

'Before he does that,' Zachary said, 'first I have to coax Consuelo into telling me if Daniel is being held at the stronghold.'

'Want me to go with you?' Joshua said.

'Be prepared if you go,' Celia warned, 'that when you return I shall cut off your *cajones* with Lincoln's knife.'

Joshua flinched.

'Don't worry, *hermano*,' Zachary said. 'This is one job I have to do on my own.' He winked and lowered his voice.

''Least you know she loves you.' Grinning, he untied his bedroll and spread it on the ground.

Joshua went to spread out his wife's bedroll but she snatched it away from him and spread it out herself. Rebuffed, he joined Macahan and Lincoln who were still squatted beside the fire, staring at the flames.

'I don't know what's wrong with her,' he said. 'I can't do anything right anymore.'

'Be patient, little brother. It ain't you she's angry at.'

'She used to like me to help her — used to thank me for it, in fact.'

'She will, again. Once Daniel's safe and we've taken care of Scar, she'll get back to being her old self.'

'I hope so,' Joshua said. 'It's getting so I hate to even talk to her for fear of causing an argument.'

Off in the darkness the wolves were howling again.

'Good news for you, Macahan,' said Lincoln.

'Yeah?'

'The brothers have eaten.'

'You can tell that by their howling?'

'Yes. Each howl has a different meaning.'

'Hallelujah,' Macahan said.

Joshua pointed at Lincoln's knife. 'I've been meaning to ask you. Where'd you get that? I've never seen one like it before.'

'A British big game hunter, Lord Gravesend, gave it to me.'

'Can I look at it?'

'Some other time,' Macahan said.

The Apache hesitated then drew the knife from its sheath and handed it to Joshua. The thick blade was about a foot long, curved, and much broader toward the leaf-shaped end.

'Heavy,' Joshua said, hefting it.

'It has to be,' said Lincoln. 'The Gurkhas use it as an all-purpose knife, a combination axe, knife, and hammer.'

'Gurkhas?'

'Men of Nepal.'

'Nepal's next to India,' Macahan

said. ''Case you didn't know.'

'Thanks, but I did go to school, remember?' Returning the knife to Lincoln, Joshua indicated two miniature knives stuck in the top edge of the wooden, goat-skin-covered sheath. 'What are they, skinning knives?'

'This one, called karda,' Lincoln said, pointing at the smaller of the tiny knives, 'is for skinning. The other, chakmak, I use to burnish the big blade.' He drew the blade lightly across his thumb, drawing blood and then slid the knife back in its sheath.

'Why'd you do that?'

'It's a Gurkha tradition,' Macahan said. 'Once the knife is drawn he can't put it back without drawing blood. That's why I didn't want him to show it to you.'

'Sorry, I didn't know,' Joshua said. The Apache shrugged as if to say it wasn't a problem. Joshua stood there another moment feeling awkward, then said goodnight and returned to his bedroll.

Macahan watched as his brother flopped down beside Celia. 'He's a good kid.'

'I can tell that,' Lincoln said.

'Still a bit green behind the ears, but . . . honest and loyal as the day is long.'

'Just like a certain deputy sheriff I once knew. Young chap. Jolly good sort and all that rubbish.'

'Aw, Judas, not that awful accent again.'

'Tried to arrest me once for drinking in a bar in Lordsburg.'

'How was I supposed to know you were the only Apache in the whole of New Mexico who didn't drink?'

'Quite. Quite. Perfectly understandable, old chap. After all, first day on the job and all. How could you possibly tell the difference between mescal and a pink strawberry soda?'

'Shut up,' Macahan said. 'Just shut the hell up.'

17

When Macahan woke the next morning the last of the stars were still out. The silvery pre-dawn dew had soaked everything, making it look as if it had rained. He shivered and retreated under his glistening poncho. He was dozing off when he heard a noise. Poking his head out, he saw that the Apache was already dressed and stirring the embers to get them blazing under the coffee pot.

'I could use a mug of that, *amigo*.'

'I'll trade you for a readyroll.'

Macahan dug a flat tin box out of his shirt pocket, opened it, and took out one of Joshua's readyrolls. He handed it to Lincoln who gave him a mug of coffee. Macahan sipped it while the Apache fired his smoke.

Macahan then lit his own readyroll from the same burning stick. He inhaled. Exhaled. Sighed with pleasure. Looked at his readyroll and grinned. 'Ain't progress a beautiful thing?'

'For some,' said Lincoln. 'Not so much for my people.'

'They could have left the reservation and come down here like you did.'

'They chose not to run away from their families.'

'Sounds like you regret you did.'

'Every moment of every day.'

'Could always go back,'

'No one can go back.'

'Can't live with regret all your life either.'

'Don't you?'

'Prudence?'

'If you had the chance again, wouldn't you marry her?'

'Not if Texas fell into the Gulf.'

'That's what I thought,' grinned the Apache. Rising, he went to his mustang and swung up on the roan's bare back.

'*¿A donde vas?*' Macahan said.

'*A ver como estan los lobos.*'

'Well, while you're checking on your doggies give 'em a hug for me.'

* * *

After breakfast Celia and Joshua gave Zachary all the money they had with them. Seeing how concerned they looked, he gripped them fondly by the shoulders and told them not to worry. Everything was going to be fine.

'But what if this Consuelo woman doesn't know if Daniel's there?' said Joshua. 'I mean what if Scar's men haven't told her?'

'Now who's being pessimistic?' Zachary said. He hugged his brother and kissed Celia on the cheek. 'I'll be back soon with good news.'

'*Vaya con Dios*,' Celia said.

Zachary grinned. 'Thanks, but I'm not sure God would be comfortable where I'm going.' He walked over to Macahan who stood holding their horses.

'I'll ride with you aways,' Macahan said.

'Think I'm going to abscond with their money?'

'With you, I never know what to think.'

They followed a deer trail out of the scrub- and cacti-covered hills. Ground squirrels scurried across their path and bright orange and blue butterflies flitted amongst the brush.

'What did you want to talk to me about?' Zachary said.

'Why Colonel Slocum lied about your escape.'

'What makes you think he did?'

'Don't waste my time stalling. Just answer the goddamn question.'

Zachary sighed, resigned, and carefully chose his words. 'He had to.'

'Go on.'

'I can't tell you any more.'

'Can't or won't?'

'Can't.' He reined up. Macahan did the same. 'All I can say is this,' Zachary said. 'If you'll play along with me on this, you won't be sorry.'

'I'm already sorry,' Macahan said.

Wheeling the bay around, he dug his spurs in and galloped back the way he'd come.

When Macahan rode into camp he noticed the Apache had not returned. Dismounting, he tied his horse to the tether line and joined Joshua and Celia at the fire.

Celia handed him a mug of steaming coffee. Thanking her, he hunkered down, took out papers and tobacco and rolled a smoke. It was a habit, something he always did when he was undecided about something; like a cat pausing to lick itself before it decided if it should drink its milk or chase a mouse. No one spoke, No one even looked at each other. They were too busy trying to hold their emotions together. A flock of crows flew overhead, cawing.

'If it's this awful for us,' Joshua said, speaking to the fire. 'How awful must it be for a small, helpless boy?' His voice choked and tears glistened in his eyes.

Celia pressed her hand over his. She

wanted to reassure him but she didn't trust herself to speak.

'He won't have to live with it much longer,' Macahan said grimly. 'That's one good thing.'

Shortly, they heard a horse approaching. Joshua reached for his rifle but Macahan recognized the light step of the mustang and shook his head. Moments later Lincoln rode in. The front of his shirt was torn and there was blood on his hands and on the handle of his kukri. Vaulting from the roan, he went straight to his knapsack and pulled out a clean gray shirt.

'Judas, what happened to you?' Macahan said.

'Me and my doggies fought over breakfast.'

'I'm serious, dammit.'

'Three less Villistas to fight . . . ' Lincoln spoke matter-of-factly but when he took off his shirt there was a bloody gash on his left shoulder.

'*Dios Mio*,' exclaimed Celia. 'You're hurt.' Jumping up, she went to him and examined the wound. Macahan and Joshua joined them.

'Scar's men?' Macahan said.

Lincoln nodded.

'You killed three of them?' Joshua said, slightly awed.

'Two.'

'Let me guess,' Macahan said. '*Los lobos* chewed up the third?'

'We would not be talking if they hadn't.'

'I knew I should've shot 'em,' Macahan said. But he was smiling as he spoke and even the stoic Apache managed a wry grin.

'Never mind the jokes,' Celia said. 'We have to wash that wound before it gets infected. Bring me a canteen, Josh, please.'

Joshua obeyed and Lincoln sat on a rock while Celia tore a sleeve from his shirt and washed the blood away.

'Here,' Macahan said, 'pour some of this on it.' He handed Celia a bottle of iodine. She removed the stopper. 'This may hurt,' she said to Lincoln. He nodded but showed no reaction as she poured iodine over the wound.

'Where'd you run into 'em?' Macahan said.

'Mile or so from here. I heard them talking as they rode toward me.'

'Did you catch what they said?'

'Only that they had spent the night drinking and whoring in the village,' He looked meaningfully at Macahan. 'There may be others.'

'Christ on the cross,' Macahan breathed.

'What, what?' said Joshua.

'Looks like Consuelo had a busy night.'

For a moment it didn't sink in. Then Joshua said: 'My God — Zachary!'

'Easy,' Macahan said. 'He can take of himself.'

'You don't think we should go help him?'

'We don't know he needs help.'

'And if he does?'

'We're already too late.'

'So that's it? We just forget about him?'

'We wait, is all.'

'Sounds like you don't give a hoot.'

'Don't be a damn fool.'

'No, no, I mean it,' Joshua said. 'You've always envied Zach. Maybe even hated him.'

'That's a lie. I just didn't put him on a pedestal like you did.'

'That isn't it, and you know it. You dislike him because he always did what he wanted and now you don't care what happens to him.'

'I care,' Macahan said quietly. 'We lose him and our chances of rescuing Daniel go down a notch.'

'I meant — as a brother.'

'I know what you meant.'

Joshua cracked. He swung on his brother, a quick hard right that caught Macahan by surprise. He went sprawling.

Instantly the Apache jumped between them.

'¡No! ¡Basta!' Celia screamed, and pulled Joshua away.

'Go ahead, stick up for him,' he said

sullenly. 'I see the way you two look at each other.'

Celia slapped him.

Joshua went white. He started to retaliate then dropped his hand. He glared at his wife and saw the shame in her dark, flashing eyes. It was like a stab in the heart. Turning away, he glared down at Macahan. 'What they say about you — I never believed it till now. You *are* a cold, heartless son of a bitch.' He stormed off.

Rising, Macahan gingerly rubbed his jaw, testing to see if it was broken.

'*¿Estas bien?*' Celia said.

'*Si.*'

'*Cuanto lo siento.*'

'*Olvidalo. Estoy bien*. I mean it,' he added when she looked doubtful. 'I'm fine. Forget it.'

'Josh didn't mean it, you know. He's just upset.'

'I know that.'

'He loves you and admires you. It's just . . . he's so torn apart by what's happened to Daniel that he barely knows what he's doing.'

'It's okay,' Macahan said gently. 'I understand.'

'If anyone's to blame, it's me. I made him feel like the kidnapping was his fault — '

Suddenly a horse whinnied. They whirled around and saw Joshua stepping into saddle.

'Josh! Josh, wait!' Macahan ran toward his brother. But Joshua ignored him and galloped out of the camp.

Macahan started for his horse but the Apache had already swung up on the mustang and, jerking it around, raced after Joshua.

'Damn fool,' Macahan said. 'Doesn't he know these hills are crawling with Villistas?'

'Hopefully,' Celia said, 'he will come to his senses before they see him.'

'For Daniel's sake, you better hope so. The only advantage we got is surprise. Scar finds out we're here and . . . ' he left the rest of the sentence unsaid.

190

Celia didn't say anything. Her whole world seemed to be crumbling around her. In her agitated state she looked at Macahan and saw him as the only person she could count on. Moving close to him, she looked up into his strong, lined, rugged face and expressed how she felt about him with her eyes.

He reddened. 'What Josh said . . . about the way I look at you . . . I apologize for that.'

'That's not what he said. He said the way 'we' look at each other.'

Macahan reddened even more. 'Any way you slice it, I was wrong. Wrong as a man can get. And you got my word, it stops right now.'

'What if I don't want it to stop?'

'That's crazy talk. You love my brother, and I know he loves you.'

'I also love *you*.'

'No, you don't. This is just a bad time and you need someone to lean on.'

'That's not what I'm feeling right now.'

'You got to stop talkin' like that. It

don't do either of us any good.'

Somewhere deep inside her, Celia sensed he was right; but it did not matter. Despite her frantic need to get her son back or, perhaps because of it, she could not control her emotions; and although she knew it was wrong, she desperately wanted Macahan to hold her; to hold her and love her and tell her that he would make everything all right. Grasping his arms, she put them around her; and when he tried to pull them away, she held them there.

'Can you honestly say you don't love me?' she asked softly.

'Y-Yes.'

'Yes?'

'Yes.' He pulled his arms free before adding: 'If I do love you, it's like a sister.'

Celia smiled, faintly mocking. '*Nuingun hombre a visto a su hermana de la manera que tu me miras a mi.*'

Macahan knew she was right. He was a man and hadn't been looking at her like she was his sister. Celia's voice broke into his thoughts.

'Is it not possible to love two men at once?' she said.

'No.'

'You don't sound so sure.'

He wasn't. But he didn't want her to know that.

'It's got to stop. That's all there is to it.'

'¿Yo pregunto?' she said.

Macahan wondered, too.

18

After twenty minutes or so the two of them came riding into camp. The wolves trotted behind them like a ghostly escort. But they stopped just short of camp and stood there in the middle of the sandy trail, tongues lolling, the wind ruffling their fur, yellow eyes fixed on the Apache, as if undecided about what to do next. One sat and scratched its ear. The other playfully charged it, knocking it off its feet. It regained them almost instantly and for several moments they fought and tumbled and gently chewed on each other; then, almost faster than the eye could follow, both wolves sprang apart and ran off into the brush.

In camp, Celia stood by the horses, feeding her dun a handful of grain. She did not look at her husband but her relief that he was safe was evident.

Hunkered down by the fire, drinking coffee and smoking, Macahan looked up as they rode past and caught Lincoln's eye. The Apache nodded, assuring him all was well. Relieved, Macahan dumped out his coffee and went to his bedroll. He rinsed out the cup with water from his canteen, put the cup in his saddle bag, and carefully fastened the strap. It was all done methodically, with no trace of emotion. If he had been sitting in a pew in church he could not have looked more relaxed. But inwardly his guts were churning.

Dismounting, Joshua and the Apache tied their horses to the tether line. Joshua was calmer, but miserable. His boyish face looked drained. Ignoring Macahan, he walked over to Celia and kissed her on the cheek. Though angry at him for running off, she was so relieved that he was back safely that she managed to control her temper and gave him a faint smile. Acting as if nothing was wrong, he told her that

Lincoln's wound needed attention. It was bleeding again. He watched her hurry to the Apache, wishing she was that attentive to him. Loosening the saddle cinch under his horse's belly, he went to the fire, took the pot from the dying embers, and poured himself a mug of coffee.

'It needs stitches,' Celia told Lincoln after examining his wound. 'Otherwise it will just break open every time you exert yourself.'

'I got a needle and thread,' Macahan said.

'Bring the iodine again, too,' she said.

'And the brandy,' Lincoln said.

'Just what we need,' Macahan grumbled. 'A drunken Injun on our hands.'

No one laughed.

After Celia finished stitching up the wound, she returned the needle and thread to Macahan. 'I can bandage it,' she told the Apache, 'but it will heal faster if the air gets to it.'

Lincoln nodded, thanked her, and started to button up his shirt.

'Wait,' Celia indicated the medallion hanging from a strip of rawhide around the Apache's neck. 'What is that, some sort of medal?'

'It's *the* medal,' Macahan said.

'Shut up,' Lincoln said. 'It is nothing, senora.'

'Don't believe him. He's just being modest.'

'I'm warning you, Macahan. Shut your face.'

Macahan grinned. 'Tell her how you won it, Linc.'

The Apache glared at him and continued buttoning his shirt.

'He beat General Crooke at checkers ten times in a row.'

'Let me see that.' Joshua approached and looked closely at the medallion. Though it was old and worn smooth in places, he recognized an eagle perched above two cannons and a cluster of cannon balls. Below the balls was a wreath of thirty-four stars surrounding Minerva. The goddess was holding a shield as she fended off Discord, who was represented by snakes.

'Holy Christ,' Joshua said, humbled. He turned to Macahan, adding: 'Now I know what you meant.'

'Will someone tell me what you're talking about,' Celia said.

'It's the Medal of Honor,' Joshua said. 'The highest military decoration that the government can award.'

Celia looked at the medal and then at Lincoln, equally awed. 'Forgive me. I had no idea.'

The Apache squirmed and said nothing.

'He'll never tell you,' Macahan said, 'but he won it for valor fighting against the Chiricahuas. Ain't that right, *amigo*?'

'I hope you rot in hell,' Lincoln said.

'You're the second person who's told me that this week. Must be a consensus of opinion.'

Joshua stood at solemn attention. 'I salute you, sir,' he said, and saluted the Apache.

Lincoln looked embarrassed. Giving

Macahan a final glare, he finished buttoning his shirt, and stalked off.

'Reckon there'll be no livin' with him now,' Macahan said.

'Stop teasing him, Ezra,' Celia said. 'Can't you see he doesn't like it —' She broke off, alarmed, as shots were fired in the distance. As one they all looked in the direction of Janos.

'Zach!' said Joshua.

* * *

Led by Macahan, they spurred their horses to the edge of the hills. Riding flat-out across the plain toward them was Zachary. He was bent low over the neck of his golden stallion, easily out-running a dozen or so pursuing Villistas. Realizing they could not catch him, they reined up and emptied their rifles at him.

Remembering all too well that he'd lost Lady under similar circumstances Macahan dismounted, rested his Winchester on a rock, aimed carefully, and fired. A Villista threw up his hands and fell backward off his horse. Macahan picked off two more in rapid succession. By then Joshua, Celia, and the Apache were also firing. Three more Villistas toppled from their saddles. The remaining men whirled their mounts around and raced back to the village.

Macahan grimly turned to the others. 'Reckon we can kiss surprise goodbye.'

★ ★ ★

'What happened?' Macahan said when Zachary reined up beside them in the foothills. 'Did you talk to Consuelo?'

Zachary nodded and quickly explained that he had been in the back room of the cantina with her, drinking tequila, when suddenly three Villistas staggered in. 'They were skunk-drunk and looking to bed her. She'd just admitted that Scar had kidnapped a gringo boy from Columbus and was keeping him at the hacienda, but as soon as she saw the Villistas she clammed up and started fawning over them. I knew one of them from Chihuahua when we were both riding with Villa. He wasn't as drunk as the other two, and I think I could have talked my way out of there. But they must have heard us talking because one pulled a knife and before I could stop him, threatened to cut Consuelo's throat. '*¡Traidor! ¡Apestoso traidor!*' he yelled at her. Of course she panicked . . . began screaming that I'd forced her to talk about *La Marcada Uno* and the kidnapping . . . and I had no choice then but to shoot my way out of there.'

'But she definitely said Acosta has Daniel?' Joshua said.

'Yep.'

'With him at his stronghold?' Celia said.

'Yes. But here's the funny thing. Moments before the Villistas busted in, I'd asked her about the ransom and why Scar hadn't demanded any money for the boy's release. She looked at me like she had no idea what I was talking about.'

201

'Why would she lie about that?' Macahan said.

'I don't think she was lying.'

'The men must not have told her about it,' Joshua ventured.

'That's one answer.'

'And the other?'

Zachary shrugged. 'She genuinely didn't know about it. Which I find odd.'

'Why?' Macahan asked.

'Because Consuelo knew everything else about the kidnapping. Said according to one of his men, Scar had planned it before Villa decided to attack Columbus. Said he intended to cross the border to get Daniel months before the raid, but Villa ordered him not to; said it might tip off the Army at Camp Furlong.'

There was silence.

'Did she actually say 'Daniel'?' Macahan said.

'Yes. And that's another odd thing. The way she described it, she made it sound like Scar *knew* Daniel.'

'That's absurd,' Celia said. 'How

202

could he possibly know Daniel?'

'Beats me,' said Zachary. He shrugged. 'I'm probably reading too much into it. Most likely just a case of too much tequila. When I got there, she was already hung over from drinking all night with other Villistas — '

'That must be it,' Celia said.

Joshua, who'd been quiet up till then, said: 'No, there has to be something else.'

'What makes you say that?' asked Macahan.

'Because there are other families — families with fathers, officers for instance, who earn much more than I do. In fact, one officer, Lt. Wyant, comes from a rich family and has three children. So why kidnap the son of a lowly corporal when you could demand ten times more from him or, say, a major or even a colonel?'

There was another silence as his words sunk in.

'I never thought of that,' Macahan admitted. 'Good thinking, Josh.'

'It must be on account of my father,' Celia said. 'Before Huerta's vultures stole everything from him, he was a wealthy man. Perhaps Acosta thought I inherited some of his money.'

'Now that makes sense,' Zachary said. 'Because you're right, *hermano*. If you're looking for a big payday, you wouldn't expect to get it from a corporal.'

'Macahan,' Lincoln said.

'What?'

'It is time we rode.'

'He's right,' Macahan said. 'By now Scar knows we're here and what we're after. We got to make it to his stronghold before he can ambush us in the hills.'

'I have a suggestion,' said Joshua,

Macahan looked at his kid brother, who seemed to have matured in the hours since their fracas. 'Make it fast.'

'Won't Acosta be expecting us to do exactly that?'

'Most likely, yeah.'

'Then let's fool him.'

'What do you have in mind?' Zachary said.

'Well, I don't know the terrain like you do, and maybe what I'm suggesting isn't possible — '

'Get to the meat,' Macahan said.

'Let's swing north or south, depending which is easiest on the horses, and work our way around to the rear of the stronghold.'

'¿La Escalera del Diablo?'

'Why not? The Devil's Stairway is where Ez wants to cause the diversion. And you said yourself Scar doesn't bother to post lookouts there. Why not start from there instead of going in the front door and then having to split up and send Lincoln around back by himself?'

Zachary looked at Macahan. 'Means tackling the lower slopes of the Sierras. Could take us an extra day.'

'Not if we rode all night,' the Apache said.

Macahan unconsciously glanced at Celia.

'Don't put this on me,' she snapped. 'If you can ride all night, so can I. Longer, if necessary.'

Macahan weighed his options for another moment; then he nodded. 'We'll do it. Well done, Josh.'

'Just trying to earn my wages,' Joshua said. Without looking at Celia or waiting for the others, he nudged his horse forward and headed back up the trail.

Lincoln and Celia rode after him.

'Seems to me,' Zachary said, 'our kid brother just sprouted wings.'

'All it takes is a poke in the jaw,' Macahan said. He kicked the bay into a trot and rode after the others, leaving Zachary puzzled.

19

They rode for the rest of the day and much of that night, stopping only to water and rest the horses and the pack-mule and to relieve themselves. They ate and drank in the saddle. The going was difficult and treacherous. Often, a misstep threatened to send horse and rider plunging down a slope into a ravine. The hills grew steeper and more rocky, the narrow winding trails often covered with dense, prickly vegetation. Then there was the broiling sun, relentlessly pounding down on them. And ahead, always towering ominously over them, were the rock- and brush-covered peaks of the Sierra Madre Occidental. Only the thought of Daniel being held hostage by someone as cruel and ruthless as *La Marcada Uno* kept them going.

Toward late afternoon the Apache

rode on ahead of the others. He made no attempt to say where he was going, and neither did Macahan, so no one asked. A half-hour later Lincoln returned holding a short-limbed bow he had just made and a bundle of arrows tied with rawhide. He looked disgruntled, and when Macahan rode alongside him and asked what was wrong, the Apache grumbled about the fact that he had not been able to find any osage orange or ironwood or even hickory to make the bow and had to settle for oak, which was brittle and did not bend well. Nor did he have time to back it with sinew, giving it much more power and resiliency —

'In other words, it ain't much of a bow.'

'I have made better.'

'That's encouraging.'

'Do not worry. It will do the job.'

'It better. I'm relying on you.'

Once in a great while Macahan looked behind him. But if the wolves were following they were doing it secretively; and only after several hours, just before twilight, did he get one glimpse of them darting through the brush.

By nightfall they had skirted the lower slopes of the Sierra Madre and were within a rifle shot of the rear of stronghold. But separating them from the base of the Devil's Stairway was a dauntingly deep gorge with sheer walls of rock on both sides. Carved millions of years ago by a raging river that had long since dried up, the bottom of the gorge presented a natural obstacle course filled with a dangerous jumble of jagged rocks and gigantic boulders that looked as if they had been randomly tossed there by a maniacal giant.

'Welcome to *Canon del Infierno*,' Zachary said as they sat astride their weary mounts at the mouth of the gorge.

'If hell created it,' said Joshua, 'why is it so damn c-cold?'

'Pray that you never have to ride

through it in the heat of the day, *hermano*, or you'll live to regret that question.'

Macahan raised up in his stirrups to give his cramped legs and aching buttocks some temporary relief and looked up at the walls looming above him. By moonlight they seemed even more craggy and forbidding. Loose dirt suddenly rained down behind them. They all turned, saddles creaking, and, looking upward, caught a glimpse of the two wolves silhouetted against the inky sky. Seconds later distant howls floated down to them.

'I'm glad they're still with us,' Celia said, yawning. 'For some reason I find their presence comforting.'

They rode on into the gorge, the weary horses carefully picking their way over the stony ground. Though the pace was barely a walk, several times they stumbled on the loose shale, almost unseating their riders, only managing to regain their balance by quickly crabbing sideways. The elegant high-strung stallion ridden by Zachary suffered the most. It slipped and almost fell several times. Zachary did his best to keep it afoot, but finally he dismounted and, reins in hand, led the skittish stallion along the easiest path he could find. Macahan rode beside him. Though exhausted, Zachary did not complain. He loved the leggy golden horse and was glad to be riding it again. He told Macahan that he'd wanted it from the first time he'd seen it prancing around at a ranch near Cuauhtemoc. The *hacendado* who owned it, had bought it as a stud for his brood mares and, as a result, the stallion had been pampered and was not used to roughing it. Macahan, who didn't believe one word of his brother's story, asked him who he'd stolen it from.

'I did not steal him,' Zachary said. 'Cognac was a gift.'

'Like hell he was.'

'Well, actually it was more like a bribe.'

'Go on.'

'The *Hacendado's* daughter became smitten with me and — '

'Her father bought you off with the stallion,' said Macahan. 'Judas! Now it all makes sense. Where you been keeping him all this time?'

'In a corral.'

'Where?' When Zachary didn't answer, Macahan said: 'You heard me. Where was the corral?'

'Behind Consuelo's cantina.'

Macahan rolled his eyes. 'Why ain't I surprised?'

'Because, brother mine, despite our differences you know me better than anyone else. And I meant that as a compliment.'

'I'll take you at your word. But all I can say is it's lucky for you the Good Lord made women, or you'd never make it through life.'

'Amen, brother.'

Behind them the pack-mule slipped and went to its knees. Its braying bounced off the rocky cliffs, echoing in

212

the darkness. Everyone reined up.

'Maybe we should wait until day-light,' Celia said, 'before one of the horses breaks a leg.'

Macahan turned to Zachary. 'When we reach the Devil's Stairway how much farther is it to the entrance of the stronghold?'

'Not far — two miles at most. But distance isn't the problem. It's the difficulty of the trail once we get past the Stairway that will slow us down. It climbs almost straight up the side of the canyon for about half a mile then levels off and gets so narrow there's barely enough room for one horse to walk. After that, it winds past several drop-offs before finally descending to the entrance.'

'Drop-offs?' Celia said.

'Five or six hundred feet straight down.'

'You don't like heights?' Macahan said.

'She's terrified of them,' Joshua said.

'Then stay behind. Wait at the foot of

the Stairway for Linc to get back with the dynamite. You can help him tie the sticks to his arrows — '

'I am not staying behind,' Celia said firmly. '*Que es definitiva.*'

'Honey,' Joshua began.

'Final,' she repeated. 'Let us not speak of this matter again.'

Macahan shrugged. Stubbornness had been a big issue between him and Prudence and long before she left him he'd learned that no matter how much he argued, she never gave in.

'Let's ride,' he said.

20

Even more massive and awe-inspiring in the moonlight, the Devil's Stairway rose vertically before them for almost a thousand feet. The gigantic slabs of stone, spewed out by a volcano before even dinosaurs roamed the earth, lay piled atop one another like a mountain of broken steps.

Macahan reined in the bay and looked at the sky above him. Though still indigo, there was a faint tinge of pale yellow forming in the eastern horizon. Dawn was only about two hours off, and he knew they were going to have to push themselves to reach the entrance before daylight. 'You go on ahead,' he told the Apache. 'You can make better time without us.'

Lincoln nodded. Dismounting, he handed the reins to Macahan and looped his bow and the bundled

215

arrows over his head so that they rested on top of his empty backpack. Then shaking his shoulders to make sure they did not rattle when he moved, he grabbed his Winchester from its scabbard, and jogged up the trail. Two dark shapes materialized out of the darkness and loped silently after him.

Macahan turned to Zachary: 'You know the trail. You lead.'

His brother nodded and looked at Joshua and Celia. 'The horses won't make it all the way to the top, so be prepared to dismount when I signal.' He urged the skittish stallion on up the trail.

Joshua and Celia followed. They hadn't said much to each other since Joshua had punched his brother but as they rode past Macahan, he could see no trace of anger on their faces. Hoping they had made up, he fell in behind them.

* * *

The trail climbed curving up the outer wall of the canyon. Though steep and flanked on both sides by jagged rocks, the trail was firm and the horses had no trouble at first. Even the mule, usually resistant to any type of incline, plodded meekly along at the end of its rope.

As Macahan rode ever upward, one hand gripping the horn to keep him from falling backward, he went over the plan in his mind. Once the Apache stole the dynamite and climbed up the ridge behind the hacienda, he was to tie the sticks to his arrows, light the fuses, and start shooting randomly into the canyon. He was not to aim near the hacienda for fear of harming Daniel, but if he could hit the bunkhouse shown on Zachary's map and blow up most of Scar's men, so much the better. Hopefully the explosions would distract the lookouts and the men manning the machine guns guarding the entrance, allowing Macahan and the others to ride in, grab Daniel from the hacienda, and ride out again before Scar and his men could stop them. That was the plan and, of course, it always ended successfully in Macahan's mind. But he'd lived too long and had been bitten too often by unexpected mishaps not to expect something unforeseen to go wrong. If one happened, he thought grimly, they would just have to overcome it. All that mattered was the final outcome; and the final outcome in this case was getting Daniel away from Acosta and safely back home with his folks.

After thirty minutes or so, the angle of the climb became so steep that Zachary reined up and signaled for everyone to dismount. 'It gets slippery from here on,' he warned, 'so watch your step.'

Macahan waited for the others to get started; then bent almost double, he scrambled upward. The mule and the horses grudgingly followed.

Each laboring step became a painful effort. Macahan felt his lungs burning and his throat grow parched. To make matters worse the ground underfoot was now partly shale and loose stones showered down on him. He kept slipping and falling to his knees. Once he lost his footing altogether and slithered back down the slope for several feet until he was able to grasp a rock and stop himself. Ahead, Joshua and Celia were experiencing the same problem; twice Celia's feet slid out from under her and each time Joshua grabbed her legs, preventing her from sliding back down the slope.

Finally, the trail leveled off. The four of them stood there for a few moments, gasping for air. Zachary seemed more concerned about the stallion than himself. During the climb it had twice gone to its knees and now its lower legs were bloody. He wanted to stop and check its wounds, but Macahan wouldn't let him. 'We don't have time to baby that horse,' he said gruffly. 'We don't make it to the entrance by the time Linc starts shooting his arrows, he will have risked his life for nothing.'

For an instant it looked as if Zachary might argue; then, reluctantly, he led them on along the narrow trail.

The sky began to lighten behind the mountains in the east.

'How much farther?' Macahan asked.

'We're nearly to the drop-offs,' said Zachary. 'Once we get past them safely, it's no more than ten minutes before we begin the descent.'

Macahan looked down into the darkness hiding the steep, rocky slope to his left and wondered how much more dangerous the trail would get. His answer awaited him around the next curve: here, splashed by moonlight, the trail was no more than two feet wide and its left edge plunged straight down for six hundred feet into a gorge. After about ten yards the trail widened again for a short distance and then repeated the process two more times.

'Keep moving,' Macahan said gently as Celia froze. 'One slow step at a time. And don't look down.'

Too fearful to reply, she flattened

herself against the inner wall, closed her eyes until they were slits, and inched forward.

Ahead of her, Zachary led the stallion past the first drop-off. The jittery horse gave him no problem and they passed it safely. 'Good boy,' he said, rubbing its muzzle. 'Only two more and we're home safe and sound.' He led the stallion forward. It seemed fine. But after a few steps it suddenly balked and fearfully jerked its head back. Almost pulled off his feet, Zachary flattened against the wall, his boots kicking a shower of loose shale over the precipice. 'Easy, easy,' he whispered. 'Whoa . . . Easy now, boy.'

'Cover its eyes,' Macahan said. 'What it can't see it can't be scared of.'

Zachary waited until the horse had calmed down then unknotted his bandanna.

Celia, Joshua and Macahan stood with backs pressed against the inner wall, a dew-soaked breeze dampening their faces, while Zachary gently tied the bandanna over the stallion's eyes. 'It's okay,' he soothed, stroking the trembling horse. 'I'm right here. Nothing to be scared — '

The stallion took a nervous step forward, felt the ground slide away under its hoof and reared back. Zachary felt himself pulled off his feet. Forced to let go of the reins, he watched, horrified, as the panicked horse tried to regain its footing, failed, and plunged over the cliff.

Celia gasped and covered her face with her hands. For an instant she swayed, dangerously close to the edge.

Macahan started forward to help her; then stopped as Joshua dropped his reins, grasped his wife and pulled her back. He whispered something to her that seemed to comfort her.

'Let's keep moving,' Macahan said gently.

'I can't,' Celia said.

'Sure you can,' Joshua said.

'*No, no, no puedo. No puedo. Tengo que volver.*'

'You can't go back,' Joshua said. He stroked her head fondly, 'There's no room for the horses to turn around.'

She muttered something under her breath that no one understood.

'Trust me,' Joshua said. 'I swear I won't let anything happen to you.'

'If you go back now,' Zachary said, 'Cognac will have died for nothing.'

Celia, hands still over her face, didn't reply.

'Think of Daniel,' Macahan said. 'He's counting on you — you and Josh — to take him home. Don't want to disappoint him, do you?'

Celia slowly lowered her hands. She looked fearfully at Joshua. Reminding her to keep looking straight ahead, he cupped his hands about her waist and guided her along the narrow trail past the precipice. Once the trail widened, he stopped and pressed her back against the rock. 'Don't move,' he said.

She clutched his hand. 'D-Don't leave me.'

'I won't. I'm just going to get the horses.'

'N-No.'

'I'll only be two seconds. Now, stay put.' He gently pulled his hand free and started back to the horses.

At the rear, Macahan watched as Joshua led first Celia's horse and then his own past the drop-off up to his wife. At that moment he was prouder of his younger brother than he'd ever been.

'Take Zach's hand,' Joshua told Celia. 'I'll be right behind you.'

'No,' she said. She turned to Zachary. 'Please, you take the horses. I feel safer with Josh.'

He nodded and squeezing past in front of her, took the reins from his brother. Joshua joined his wife and guided her past the other two precipices onto wider ground. 'See, nothing to it,' he grinned.

She was trembling too hard to answer.

Macahan and Zachary now joined them with the other horses and the pack mule. 'From here on,' Zachary said, 'it's all level until we hit the descent.'

Macahan glanced at the ever-lightening sky. 'We better go like hell. Another twenty minutes and the lookouts will be able to see us.'

'Don't worry. They won't be looking this way. It's only when we're on the valley floor by the mouth of the canyon that we'll be sitting ducks.'

'By then,' Macahan said, 'hopefully Linc will be blasting 'em with dynamite.'

'Amen, brother.'

21

In the pre-dawn light the entrance to the horseshoe-shaped canyon looked exactly as Zachary described it. Two jagged, hundred-foot lime-stone cliffs formed an upside-down triangle, with the upper part about sixty feet apart and the ground level barely wide enough to drive a wagon through. He had also accurately described the machine gun posts. There was one dug into the rocks of both cliff-tops. Each tripod-mounted .303 caliber Maxim machine gun was manned around the clock by three shifts of Scar's most loyal men who climbed to their posts by rope ladders. To ensure security, the men on duty did not lower the ladders until it was time to change shifts.

But what Zachary had neglected to describe was the massive net made out of 3-inch-thick rope entwined with barbed-wire that hung down from the top blocking anyone from entering.

From behind a rocky outcrop facing the entrance, Macahan and the others stared at the rope net in shocked silence. Finally Zachary found his voice. 'It must be new,' he said. 'I never would've forgotten something like that.'

'We'll have to cut our way through,' Joshua said.

'Won't be time,' Macahan said. 'Linc only has about a dozen arrows. Even if he finds enough dynamite for each arrow, it'll only take him a few minutes at most to shoot them. By then, without heavy wire cutters, we wouldn't be able to cut a hole big enough to crawl through, let alone ride a horse through. We'd be fodder for the machine guns.'

'Which means we either have to find a way to raise the net or blast through it,' Zachary said.

Macahan looked up at the sky. It was more yellow than gray now, indicating dawn was only minutes away. 'Forget about raising the net. Even if one or two of us could make it to the top of the cliffs without being seen, by then it'll be broad daylight.'

'What about Lincoln?' Celia said.

'What about him?'

'Couldn't we signal to him to shoot one of his arrows at the net and blow a hole in it for us?'

'It's a good idea,' Macahan said, 'except again, there won't be time. Even if he sees our signal, whatever that is, he'd have to work his way along the ridge to get within arrow range. By then it would be past sunup. Also we've got to be riding flat-out toward the hacienda seconds after the first explosion. Otherwise, Scar will have time to grab Daniel and use him as a shield or, worse, threaten to kill him if we don't throw down our guns.'

'So what do you suggest we do,' Joshua said. 'Throw in the towel before the fight even starts?'

'I ain't suggesting nothing of the sort. I just need a moment to think, that's all.'

Everyone waited while he thought.

'All right,' he said suddenly, 'Josh, cut me off some of that dry mesquite over there. You two,' he turned to Zachary and Celia, 'unload the extra ammo from the panniers.' As the three of them followed orders, Macahan took a coil of rope from his saddle bag and tied one end to the mule's pack-harness. When Joshua returned with an armful of mesquite, Macahan tied it to the other end of the rope. By then Celia and Zachary were stuffing their pockets, and the pockets of Joshua and Macahan, with boxes of cartridges.

'Now, what?' Joshua asked.

Macahan got out his matches and distributed them among the others. 'Soon as the first explosion hits, set fire to this dead brush.'

'You're going to burn the net?' Zachary said.

'I'm going to try,' Macahan said. 'Hanging in the sun all day it must be dry as tinder.'

'What about the barbed-wire?' said

Joshua. 'That won't burn.'

'No, but once the rope burns the wire should drop to the ground.'

'And if it doesn't?'

'That's where the mule comes in. I'll hook the wire over one of the panniers so he can drag it aside. He'll be panicked by the fire anyway so it shouldn't take much to make him bolt.'

'You're forgetting about the machine guns,' Celia said. 'They'll cut you down before you even get close to the net.'

Macahan shrugged. 'I didn't say the plan was perfect.'

'We can help,' Joshua said. He looked up at Scar's men crouched around the two cliff-top machine guns. 'We'll try to pick them off. Or at least force the bastards to keep their heads down.'

'That'll work,' Macahan said. 'Any minute now Linc should — '

At the far end of the canyon, the Apache shot an arrow off the ridge behind the hacienda. It arced gracefully through the air, the sparking fuse of the dynamite tied to it lighting its flight, and landed between the iron legs of the water tower.

Moments later the dynamite exploded. The booming roar echoed throughout the canyon, the explosion buckling the legs and bringing the huge tank crashing to the ground. Water flooded everywhere and instantly shouts of alarm came from the lookouts perched atop the canyon walls.

'Matches!' yelled Macahan. He and the others struck their matches and set fire to the dry mesquite. Once it was aflame, he whacked the mule on the rump with his Winchester. Already terrified by the fire, the startled animal ran, braying, toward the net. Ducked low, Macahan ran beside it.

Meanwhile, on top of the ridge, the Apache loosed a second arrow. His aim was true. It landed on the roof of the old wooden bunkhouse. The explosion seconds later blew the building apart, killing many of the men inside who had just awakened. Those who weren't killed or injured were stunned by the blast. They came staggering out the door in their underwear. A third arrow buried in the ground in front of them. Before the men could run, the dynamite exploded, killing or maiming most of them. A fourth arrow exploded near the corral, panicking the horses. As one, they stampeded to the gate. At the last moment the horses in front tried to stop. But the weight and momentum of the horses surging along behind them slammed them into the gate. The impact knocked down the gate and part of the attached fence, allowing the horses to run free.

At the mouth of the canyon, Macahan grabbed the mule's bridle and pulled the frightened animal close to the net. The flaming brush set fire to the dry rope nearest the ground. The fire quickly spread in all directions.

Instantly, machine gun fire poured from both posts. Bullets kicked up the dirt beside Macahan's boots while others zipped past his head. Ducking behind the terrified mule, he fired back. Seconds later the mule went down, kicking and braying, blood flowing from a dozen holes. Macahan dived behind the dying mule and continued shooting.

Behind him, hidden by the rocks, Joshua, Celia, and Zachary pumped round after round into the machine gunners, killing two and forcing the others to momentarily keep their heads down.

By now the whole rope net was ablaze. The wall of flames turned the canyon bright as day. Macahan saw the long strands of barbed-wire were turning red-hot but weren't collapsing as he had hoped. He tried to signal to the others behind the rocks but machine gunners saw him and opened fire, pinning him down.

Seeing his brother trapped, Joshua mounted up and spurred his horse to the wire. Bullets whined about his ears. Wrapping his lariat around the saddle horn, he tossed the loose end to Macahan, who knotted it around the wire, Joshua kicked up his horse and galloped back to the rocks, dragging a section of the flaming net with him.

The machine gunners swiveled the Maxim around and fired at Joshua. But the smoke and flames from the burning net hid their view of him and the bullets dug holes in the sand behind him.

Behind the rocks, Zachary yelled to Celia to follow him. Swinging up on Macahan's horse, he waited until she was mounted, then together they raced toward the burning net.

Crouched behind the dead mule, Macahan saw them coming. He kept firing at the machine gunners, keeping them pinned down until his brother got close. Then jumping to his feet, he swung up behind Zachary.

'Where's Josh?'

'Right behind us!'

Bullets zipping about their heads, they galloped after Celia.

Peppered by machine gun fire and shots from the lookouts perched along the cliff-tops, they jumped their horses through the ragged hole in the still-burning net. For a few, lung-searing moments the fire was all around them. Flames scorched their skin and singed their clothes and burned their horses' manes. Then they were safely through. Able to breath again, they galloped on into the canyon.

Joshua quickly followed them and all three horses raced toward the hacienda, bunkhouse, and a large corral located at the rear of the canyon.

High on the ridge above the hacienda, the Apache saw them coming. He tried to keep the lookouts pinned down with rifle fire. But he could not contain them all. A bullet cut down Macahan's bay. Zachary and Macahan went sprawling. Macahan was up first.

'You all right, Zach?'

Groggy, Zachary signaled that he was fine and waved his brothers on. 'Don't wait for me. Get Daniel!'

Macahan swung up behind Joshua and they galloped off after Celia.

Zachary pulled his rifle from its

scabbard and, crawling behind the dead horse, began shooting at the lookouts.

The machine gunners swung their Maxims around and opened fire at Zachary. They were deadly accurate at that range and their bullets chewed the dead horse to pieces.

The Apache, seeing Zachary pinned down, ran along the eastern ridge until he was in range of the nearest machine gun post. Taking quick aim, he shot his last arrow. It landed behind the gunners and exploded, blowing them and the Maxim, along with tons of rock, into the canyon below.

The other machine gunners fired a burst at the Apache. They missed him and an instant later their gun jammed. The men wrestled with the belt. But before they could pull it loose, two dark shapes silently sprang out of the dawn light. The startled screams from the men were cut off as the wolves ripped out their throats.

22

At the far end of the canyon, Scar's remaining men took cover behind the long arched portico of the old mission-styled hacienda. Unnerved by the explosions and the deaths of their *compadres*, they would have fled; but Acosta was crouched at one of the open windows behind them, and they knew he would shoot the first man who ran.

'*¡Disparar! ¡Disparar! ¡Matar a los gringos!*'

His enraged shouts galvanized the men into action. They opened fire at the oncoming gringos.

Joshua and Celia swerved their horses, trying to make themselves difficult targets.

'Try to get to the wall,' Macahan yelled. His brother and Celia obeyed. Reining up, the three of them quickly dismounted and dived behind the wall.

Macahan waved his hat above the wall, drawing fire from the Mexicans.

'I count seven,' he said as bullets chipped the wall above their heads.

'Eight,' Joshua said. 'There's one hidden behind the rain barrel.'

'Seven or eight or a dozen, it doesn't matter,' Celia said. 'We can't sit here shooting it out with them. We have to get Daniel.'

Macahan turned to Joshua. 'Cover me while I work my way around behind the house. If I can get inside without Scar seeing me, maybe I can find him — '

'No. I'll go,' Joshua said. 'You're a better shot than me.'

'And both of you are better than me,' a voice said behind them. They turned and saw Zachary limping toward them, rifle in hand. 'Besides,' he added. 'I have a score to settle with Acosta.'

'Score?' said Macahan.

'Yeah, the little runt turned Villa against me. Otherwise, I'd still be — '

'Living the good life with the

hacendado's beautiful daughter?'

Realizing Macahan had never believed his story, Zachary grinned ruefully. 'So I stole the horse,' he admitted. 'What's a little lie between brothers?' He winced and grabbed his side.

'*Dios Mio*, you're hurt,' Celia said. Moving close, she opened his jacket revealing his bloodstained shirt.

'That don't look good,' Macahan said.

'Hurts like hell, but I'm okay,' Zachary said. 'The bullet went right through. Lost some blood, is all. Now, the three of you cover me while I go find Daniel.'

'Too late for that.' Joshua pointed at the hacienda. They all looked and saw Scar's head poke out the front door.

'*Cabachos, ya no disparen. Tengo el nino con migo.*'

'Come ahead,' Macahan yelled. 'We won't shoot.' He and the others stood up, rifles lowered, as Manuel Acosta led Daniel out.

Celia gave a tiny gasp as she saw her

son. But before either she or Joshua could say anything, Zachary stepped over the wall and confronted Acosta.

'Let the boy go, Scar.'

'And why would I do that, gringo?'

'Because this isn't about him; it's about you and me.'

Acosta smiled mockingly, one side of his mouth twisted by his long scar. 'So ... you are still angry about Señorita Mateos.'

'I know it's petty of me,' Zachary said. 'But the thought of the woman I loved being butchered for no reason ... still riles me.'

'You must blame Francisco for her death.'

'So now you're blaming Pancho Villa for your crimes?'

'It was not my crime. I was not the one who forced the señorita and her family to face a firing squad.'

'No, but it was you who lied to Villa; it was you who made him believe Carlota's father had aligned himself with Carranza.'

'What reason would I have for doing that?'

'Jealousy. You wanted Carlota; she wanted me.'

'That is the lie of all lies.'

'You'd like everyone to believe that. But I know better. Carlota told me not long before she was killed. She turned you down. Despite all your threats you were left out in the cold. And you don't take rejection well, *enano cavron*.'

Enraged at being taunted about his size, Acosta stabbed a finger at Zachary. 'I will see to it you die very slowly, gringo.'

'I don't doubt it,' Zachary said. He dropped his rifle. 'Now, let Daniel go and we'll make the swap.'

'I have a better suggestion,' Acosta said. 'All of you throw down your weapons and I will not kill the boy.'

No one moved.

'*Juro que voy a disparar.*'

'Don't believe him,' Celia said. 'He's bluffing.'

'I don't think so,' Joshua said.

'Oh, but he is. Aren't you, Manuel?'

Macahan saw Acosta's lips angrily tighten and got ready to jerk his Colt.

'Are you willing to take that risk, Señora?'

'Why not?' Celia said. 'What father would shoot his own son?'

There was a stunned, chilling silence.

Joshua looked at his wife in open-mouthed shock.

'Celia — '

'It's all right, Josh. I know what I'm doing.'

Macahan whistled softly. 'Finally things are beginning to make sense.'

'So that's why you didn't demand any ransom,' Zachary said to Acosta. 'You intended all along to keep him.'

'He is my flesh and blood. It is my right.'

'Only till I kill you.'

Acosta smirked. *Matarle!*' he whispered.

Instantly his men raised their rifles and fired.

Zachary fell where he stood, dead

before he hit the ground.

'You son of a bitch,' Macahan said. He jerked his six-gun but didn't fire as Acosta pulled Daniel in front of him like a shield.

'Go ahead, señor — shoot!'

Tempted, Macahan finally lowered his gun.

'That is better,' Acosta said. '*¡Lanzar sus armas!*'

Grudgingly, Macahan, Joshua, and Celia dropped their guns.

'Line them up,' Acosta told his men. They obeyed, herding Macahan and Joshua and Celia against the courtyard wall.

'M-Momma,' Daniel started toward Celia only to be jerked back by Scar.

'Let him alone, you bastard!' Joshua lunged toward Acosta and was instantly clubbed to his knees by two of Scar's men.

Macahan helped him up and angrily faced Acosta. 'Better think long and hard before you do this, *amigo*. Shoot us and our government will hunt you down and hang you like the yellow-bellied little weasel you are.'

'Threats,' Acosta said. 'Always with the threats! *¡Americanos!*' He spat disgustedly. Then giving Daniel to one of his men, he strutted back and forth before his captives. 'Do you think I care about what your government does or does not do? This is Mexico — my country, not yours, gringo. Here I do as I please.'

Just then the Apache appeared around the side of the hacienda. Behind him trotted the two wolves. Unnoticed by anyone but Macahan, Lincoln moved silently up behind the Mexican holding Daniel, and swung his kukri. The heavy knife sank so deep into the man's neck, his head was almost severed. He dropped to the dirt. Lincoln grabbed Daniel before he could cry out and clamped his hand over the boy's mouth.

At the same instant the wolves sprang at two of the men covering Macahan, Joshua, and Celia. The Mexicans went sprawling, their screams quickly silenced as the wolves slashed their throats. The other men turned and ran. The wolves sprang after them and in moments brought them down. The men grappled with them, desperately trying to fight them off, but it was useless. The snarling wolves were too quick. Even bullets could not stop them. Within seconds, the men were dead.

Panicked, Acosta reached for his sidearm.

Macahan rammed his shoulder into two of Scar's men, knocking them to the ground, and dived for his Colt. He hit the dirt near where he had dropped it, rolled over and came up firing just as Acosta cleared leather.

The slug punched a hole in Acosta's chest.

He staggered back a few steps, dropped his gun, and collapsed.

Joshua meanwhile kicked the feet out from under another of Scar's men and dived on top of him, punching him senseless.

Celia ran across the courtyard toward Daniel. The Apache saw her coming and happily released her son. Daniel ran to greet his mother. As he did, Lincoln saw Acosta roll onto his side, pick up his dropped revolver and aim it at Celia. The Apache hurled his kukri at him. The big curved blade shone in the dawn light as it twirled over and over in flight.

Acosta saw it coming and tried to roll aside. He was too late. The knife struck his arm near the shoulder, severing it. Acosta screamed and lay writhing in the dirt.

Celia smiled gratefully at Lincoln and grabbed Daniel up in her arms.

Seeing their leader dying, the last of Acosta's men quickly dropped their rifles and surrendered to Joshua.

Macahan walked over to Acosta.

The Mexican looked up at Macahan and tried to speak. His lips moved feebly, but no sound came from them.

'This is for Zach,' Macahan said and shot him between the eyes.

A moment later, the Apache joined Macahan and picked up his kukri. Hunkering down, he wiped the blade in the dirt until all the blood was gone. Then he tucked the kukri in its sheath, rose, and looked at his friend.

'You heading back across the border?'

'Sooner or later.'

'I'd like to tag along.'

'Never too late to go home.'

'Don't get misty on me.'

'And you try not to get on my nerves.'

They stared stoically at each other. Anyone watching would never have known how much respect and devotion these men felt for each another.

'We got some burying to do first,' Lincoln said.

Macahan turned and spat on Acosta's corpse. 'I was figuring on leaving this garbage to the carrion.' He turned back and realized he was talking to himself.

The Apache was already on his way to the wolves. One lay dying on its side.

His brother stood over him, licking the blood from the wounds. Lincoln removed his Medal of Honor from around his neck and gently hung it around the dead wolf's ruff. The other wolf watched him with sad yellow eyes.

The Apache rose and walked off to find a shovel.

BOOK THREE

23

They buried Lt. Zachary Zebulon Macahan under a grove of cottonwoods next to the dead wolf. They covered both graves with rocks but did not plant markers as it was well known that markers encouraged grave-robbers to dig up the bodies for their boots and personal belongings. Other than that it was a fine place for a grave — grassy, shady, and within sight of the little creek that brought life to the canyon. If one had to die, Macahan thought as he got out his Bible, this place was as good as any to be buried.

Joshua, Celia, Daniel, and Lincoln looked on, heads bowed, hats in hand, while Macahan prayed over Zachary's grave. Lincoln then spoke a few words in Apache over the wolf's grave. The other wolf sat nearby, howling mournfully. He, like the Macahans, had lost a brother.

It was a sad moment for everyone, but especially Joshua. He was devastated by the loss of Zachary. His devotion to his brother went deeper than he admitted even to himself and now Zach was gone, out of his life forever; and as the others prepared to depart, Joshua could not bring himself to leave the gravesite. Asking for a few minutes alone, he stood there in the hot sun, head down, eyes closed, clutching his hat, weeping like a baby.

Feeling his pain, Celia went to him and compassionately squeezed his hand. They had not spoken since she had admitted Daniel was not his child and now he responded in anger, knocking her hand aside and refusing to look at her.

'Joshua, please, I — '

'Go away, damn you,' he said harshly. 'Leave me the hell alone.'

Stung, Celia walked away. Nearby, Macahan stood with Lincoln who was showing Daniel how to 'sign' in Apache. Celia joined him.

'I think I have lost him, Ezra.'

'Give him some time,' Macahan said. 'Right now he feels deep-down hurt and betrayed, and then to lose Zach on top of everything else . . . it ain't an easy hill to climb. But he's got sand. He'll come around.'

'I would not blame him if he didn't. We've had many quarrels during our marriage, but we have always trusted one another. Now, he may never trust me again.'

Macahan sighed. 'Might've been a tad easier if you'd told Josh right after it happened.'

'I wanted to, but I was afraid I'd lose him.'

'Lying ain't always the best solution.'

'I had to risk it, not only for the sake of our marriage but his career. He had just enlisted, and there was hope of him becoming an officer. This kind of scandal would have killed his chances. You've no idea how gossip spreads on an Army base. Josh would've had it thrown in his face every day. It would have destroyed him. Can you understand that?'

'I reckon . . . '

Celia studied him with her lovely dark eyes. 'Poor Macahan,' she said softly. 'First you love me, now you hate me.'

'Who says I hate you?'

'You do. It's in your eyes . . . your voice . . . '

'That ain't hate.'

'What, then?'

'Confusion, maybe.'

'What are you confused about?'

'You. From the first time we met I thought I had you pegged. Reading people — knowing what they will or won't do under different circumstances — is all part of being a good lawman. Read folks right and odds are you'll stay alive. Read 'em wrong and they'll be praying over you.'

'And you misread me, is that what you're saying?' When he nodded, she added: 'Tell me, what did I do so wrong that caused me to fall from grace?'

'That ain't for me to say.'

'I must know.'

Macahan shifted uncomfortably on his feet, not sure how to word what he wanted to say. 'You and Acosta . . . together . . . that's something I never would've figured.'

Celia frowned. 'Together?'

'Sharing the same bed.'

'*Dios Mio*, is that what you think? — that Manuel and I were lovers?'

'Weren't you?'

'Not if he was the last man alive on earth.'

'Then . . . ?'

'He raped me, Macahan — '

'Jesus — '

'Forced himself on me one day while I was buying flowers in Palomas.'

Macahan's face turned gray with anger.

'I begged him not to. Said I'd only been married a few days and . . . but he just laughed in my face . . . told me I should be honored that he'd chosen me. I tried to run but the marketplace was crowded. His men cornered me . . . dragged me into an alley and tore my clothes off. I screamed and fought, but there were too many of them. They held me down while he . . . he climbed on top of me and — '

'That's enough,' Macahan said.

'But I want to tell you.'

'No.'

'Please, I have to tell someone.'

'Try Josh.'

'What's the point? He'd never believe me now.'

Macahan didn't answer. Both were silent for several moments.

Finally Celia, her flushed cheeks wet with tears, said: 'Do you still think you misread me, Macahan?'

'Stop it.'

'No, I want to know.'

'Cut it out.'

'Then you do believe me?'

'Dammit, Celia — '

'I could be lying, you know — making the whole thing up so you won't hate me or think I'm a whore.'

Macahan angrily grabbed her by the shoulders and shook her, hard.

'Goddammit, woman, don't say another word!'

For a long moment she stood there, sadly defiantly — then, emotionally, she collapsed. Feeling her sag, he quickly wrapped his arm around her.

Just then Daniel came running up. 'Momma — Momma, you all right?'

Celia broke away from Macahan and hugged her son. '*Si, si, chico, estoy bien.*'

The Apache joined them, somber-faced. 'He has an important question.'

'Can't it wait?' Macahan said. The look in the Apache's solemn black eyes said 'no.' 'All right, what is it?'

'He wants to know if he will ever see his Uncle Zach again.'

'Well now, Daniel, that ain't exactly up to us. But if you're a good boy and say your prayers, I reckon most likely you will.'

'I hope so,' Daniel said. 'I didn't get a chance to thank him for saving my life.'

'I'm sure he knows how you feel. Ol' Zach, he had a knack for knowing what other folks were thinking.'

'While you're at it,' Celia said, 'you should thank your other uncles, too.' Her look included the Apache, who smiled. 'Without them, you'd still be in the hands of Señor Acosta.'

'Just knowing he's safe is thanks enough,' Macahan said.

'Don't forget your father, either,' Celia said. 'Without his help — '

'He's not my father,' Daniel said. 'He's just my pretend father.'

'That's not true,' Celia said.

'Sure it is,' said Joshua. He stood glaring at her from a few yards away. 'You, of all people, should know that.' He walked off to the horses.

Celia looked at Macahan and sadly shook her head.

'Time we were headed home,' he said.

'I'll go round up horses for you and Daniel,' the Apache said. He eyed all the corpses sprawled around them.

'Plenty to choose from.'

'I want that dappled gray belonging to Acosta,' Macahan said. 'It'll send a message to the Villistas. They all know he'd never part with that horse if he weren't dead.'

★ ★ ★

They rode unchallenged out of the canyon. Earlier Macahan had released the unarmed prisoners so they could tend to the wounded and bury the dead.

Seeing so many of her people killed distressed Celia. It was so unnecessary, she said sadly to Macahan. They had died for no good reason. These men weren't soldiers they were farmers — *campesinos* with wives and families. All they wanted to do was put food on the table. Macahan agreed. Unfortunately, he said, hunger and poverty drove men to seek rainbows that did not exist. Then Villa came along and waved a cause at them — talked them into thinking they could change their lives by changing governments. Next thing they knew, they were worse off than before.

'Mexico,' Celia said bitterly. 'It will always be as father predicted: A country where the more things change the more they stay the same.'

'Amen, brother,' Macahan said, 'as Zach would say.'

★ ★ ★

Macahan and the Apache, with the wolf loping along beside them, led the way down through the hills. Celia and Daniel followed and Joshua brought up the rear. He and Celia had rarely spoken since the flare up and by his tense, tight-lipped expression it was obvious he was not ready to forgive her.

By late-afternoon they had reached the last of the foothills and were now within sight of the rooftops of Janos. The sun had beaten on them all day and they rode slumped over, ragged, and exhausted.

'We'll make camp here,' Macahan said, reining up.

'But there's still daylight left,' Joshua protested.

'An hour at most, *hermano*. No need to push things. Daniel's ready to drop from the saddle. We stop now, get a good meal in our bellies and a night's rest and we'll be able to start early tomorrow. With any luck, we'll reach the border before sundown.'

'Another twenty minutes and we could be in Janos.'

'Where they might not treat us so kindly,' Macahan reminded. 'We just put a lot of Scar's men to rest. Chances are some of them came from around here. Might not be wise to rub it in their noses.'

'Damn them, I could use a drink.'

'*That*,' Macahan said grimly, 'is the last thing you need.'

They chose a small sheltered ravine and, while the men handled the horses, Celia and Daniel spread the bedrolls and started a fire. The rope net had eventually collapsed and burned not only the mule carcass but all of their supplies, so Macahan shot two rabbits which he skinned out and roasted on a spit while Lincoln and Joshua hunted for edible roots and berries. There was still water in two of the canteens. Knowing they could always refill them from one of the many streams and rivers, they quenched their thirst and poured what remained into a hollow in one of the rocks so the wolf could drink. It then loped off into the darkness and shortly they heard it howling mournfully to the moon.

Daniel said little during the meal, but afterward when the adults were smoking around the fire and he was preparing to bed down, he pulled his mother aside. 'Momma — '

'¿Si, chico?'

'Why did you and Daddy lie to me? If Señor Acosta hadn't told me, I would never have known who my real father was.'

'Uncle Josh didn't lie,' Macahan said. 'He didn't know.'

'How couldn't he know?'

'Because I didn't tell him,' Celia said.

'Why not?'

'Right now you're too young to understand.'

'That's what you always say when you don't want to tell me something.'

'I'll tell you another time. When we get home. Right now it's late. Way past your bedtime — '

'Señor Acosta said you lied because you didn't want me to live with him in Mexico, where I belonged.'

'You belong here with me,' Celia said. 'I'm your mother.'

'He also said you were ashamed of being Mexican and that's why you married Daddy, not him.'

'*Madre de Dios*, he is the pig of all liars! I am proud of my heritage. Proud of my family name. I would not change who I am for anything,' she glanced at

Joshua. 'Or anyone.'

'If you mean me,' he said angrily, 'you don't have to worry. I never asked you or expected you to change. I loved you for who you were. But I did expect you to tell me the truth — especially when it came to who fathered your child.'

'*¡Desgraciado!*'

'All right, that's enough,' Macahan said. He stepped between them. 'This ain't the time or place to settle your family squabbles.'

'Squabbles?' Joshua laughed disgustedly. 'Finding out your wife has been cuddled up with a Villista is a little more than a squabble.'

'You will live to regret those words,' Celia said.

'Momma, please don't fight with — '

'*¡Silencio!* We will speak no more of this.' Celia reached for his hand, but he twisted away and ran to Joshua.

'I wish you were my real father,' he said. 'I love you much more than that nasty Señor Acosta.'

'I love you, too,' Joshua said. He wanted to say more, but the words choked in his throat.

'Daniel, get over here!'

'Do I have to, Daddy?'

Joshua hesitated, saw Macahan saying 'yes' with his eyes, and nodded. 'Go,' he said kissing his son on the forehead. 'We'll talk more tomorrow. Goodnight.'

'G'night, Daddy.'

24

Macahan woke instantly to a touch on his shoulder. Squatted beside him, silhouetted against a silver dollar moon, was the Apache. 'Your brother,' he said softly, 'has chosen to leave us.'

'Damn! How long ago?'

'Long enough for me to follow him down to the plain and ride back.'

'Janos?'

The Apache nodded.

Macahan threw aside his blanket and poncho and pulled on his boots.

'Stay here and look after them,' he said, indicating Celia and Daniel sleeping nearby.

'What do I tell the woman if she wakes up?'

'Nothing.'

'She is not without brains.'

'Just say Josh and I went off to talk things over.'

'And if you do not come back?'

'Jesus! Have some faith in me, will you?'

'You once told me there was a bullet waiting for all of us.'

'I was drunk. Truth is, I aim on dying in bed. And unless you prefer to drown in your own mustang's piss, I advise you do the same.' Finished dressing, Macahan moved quietly to the tether line, untied Acosta's dappled gray, and led it off into the darkness.

The Apache squatted on his heels beside the fire. Opposite, across the glowing embers, two yellow eyes blazed sadly in the dark.

The Apache gazed into them, thinking that he too missed the other wolf.

★ ★ ★

When Macahan entered Janos the streets were silent and empty. No lights showed in the adobe hovels; nor were there any whores beckoning to him from doorways and alleys. His and the gray stallion's shadow, cast ahead of them by the platinum moonlight, was their only company.

He rode past the renovated mission church, across the dark empty plaza, down the same alley he had previously led the outlaws' horses carrying their blanket-wrapped corpses, and finally reined up outside the rear of the cantina.

Macahan looked about him. The alley was dark, silent, and empty. But not the cantina: inside, the small adobe-brick building reverberated with the voices of angry men and women yelling and jeering in Spanish. Tying the gray to the rail he drew his Colt and quietly opened the back door. It led directly into the kitchen. An old blackened kerosene lamp hanging near the stove gave off enough light to show the kitchen was empty. Moving to an inner door, Macahan inched it open and peered through the crack.

The cantina was packed with villagers. Sleepy-eyed children stood on the plank bar trying to see over the adults' heads. The tables and chairs had been moved back and everyone was gathered around a man slumped on the floor. The inner circle of men and women were beating him with clubs, shovels, and hoes. Everyone else was yelling encouragement. The mob of villagers blocked Macahan's view of the man's face, but by their angry shouts and cursing, he knew it had to be his brother.

He fired a shot at the ceiling. In the small room the noise was thunderous.

Everyone whirled around in alarm. But when they saw it was only one man — a gringo — they lost their fear and raised their weapons ready to attack him.

Macahan fired again, the bullet splintering the floor in front of the closest man. He stopped, as did everyone else, and glared at the lawman.

Wishing he had a scattergun, Macahan wagged his Colt in the faces before him and before anyone could regain their courage ordered them to step back.

No one moved.

'You heard me,' Macahan said. 'Step back!

A short, sturdy man, his hands and field clothes smeared with dirt, stepped forward and glared defiantly at Macahan.

'*Señor, no te tengo miedo.*'

'I ain't asking you to be afraid, amigo. Just to step back.'

The man did not move.

'*Ya me oistes,*' Macahan repeated. '*¡Regresate!*'

For a long, dangerous moment the man did not move.

Macahan read his eyes, and the eyes of those crowded around him.

Uncertainty was slowly dissipating their rage.

Macahan took a chance that the villagers were just angry, not evil, and holstering his Colt brushed the sturdy man aside and pushed into the crowd.

Grudgingly, the villagers let him through.

Macahan kneeled beside the man sprawled face-down on the floor. He'd been beaten senseless. Macahan rolled him over. The face that stared up at him was so bruised and bloody he barely recognized his own brother.

'*¿Que hizo para merecer que lo golpearan de esa manera?*' he said angrily to the sturdy man.

'He will not tell you what your brother did for them to beat him, señor.' A fleshy, once-pretty woman in a low-cut white blouse and flowered red skirt pushed through the crowd and confronted Macahan. 'But I will.'

Macahan studied her. 'You'd be . . . Consuelo?'

The woman looked pleased. 'You have heard of me, yes?'

'Some.'

'Bring your brother to my room. He will be safe there.' Turning to the crowd, she told them to go back to their homes. This gringo, she added, was an important lawman in the United States and to harm him would bring soldiers and much trouble to their village. Without waiting to see if they obeyed her, she turned back to Macahan and motioned for him to follow her.

★ ★ ★

Consuelo's room was attached to the back of the cantina. It had once been part of a now-demolished stable. The top of one of the stalls still protruded below the wooden rafters. There were no windows and the room was just large enough for a bed, two chairs, and an ornate oaken chest-of-drawers stolen from a rich Carranza sympathizer. The *hacendado's* gilt initials still glinted on the front of each drawer.

Consuelo lit a lamp and while Macahan gently placed Joshua on the bed she took an earthen bowl outside and filled it with water from the well. When she returned Joshua had regained consciousness and Macahan was helping him to sit up. Brushing Macahan aside, she bathed Joshua's wounds and wiped the blood away before taking a bottle of mescal from a drawer.

'Reckon he's had enough of that worm,' Macahan said. He rolled and lit a smoke and put it between his brother's cracked and swollen lips. Joshua nodded his thanks but was too ashamed to look at Macahan. Closing his eyes, he leaned back against the wall and tried to collect himself.

Macahan took a swig of mescal, grimaced as the cheap liquor burned his throat, and handed the bottle to Consuelo. She apologized for not having lime or salt and took a long swig herself.

'I'd want to thank you for your kindness.'

'*De nada.*' She looked sadly at Joshua. 'Your brother, I think he has a death wish.'

'Wouldn't surprise me none. I told him folks here might not welcome him with open arms, but it didn't stop him.'

'My people did not bother him at first.'

'Sure made up for it later.'

'By then he had made them very angry.'

'You were with him?'

'From the time he entered the cantina. I recognized him — '

''Cause he looked like Zach, you mean?'

'*Si.* He is not so handsome, I think, but there is a sweetness about him that makes a woman desire to hold him to her breast.'

'So what happened exactly?'

'I told him who I was and he bought us tequila, *mucho* tequila, and we sat and talked about how he was not sure he wanted to be a soldier and then he told me that *La Marcada Uno* had killed his brother — '

'Never mind that,' Macahan said. 'Tell me what Josh did to get everyone so riled.'

'It was the tequila talking, I think. I

tried to stop him, to warn him that many women here in Janos had husbands and sons who were Villistas. But your brother, he would not listen. He stood in the doorway shouting about how many he had killed and how many more would die from their wounds and many people in the village heard him and they told others — '

Macahan stopped her. 'I get your drift,' he said.

'It is true?' Consuelo said. 'Scar is really dead?'

''Bout as dead as he's going to get.'

Consuelo became grimly silent.

Macahan said: 'Well, thanks again for your help. Here,' he dug some silver coins from his jeans and put them on the table. 'Buy yourself a new dress.'

'I have many dresses, señor.'

'Always room in a woman's closet for one more.'

'I do not want your *dinero*.'

'Why not? You earned it.'

'It is *I*, Señor Macahan, who should be paying *you*.'

'How you figure that?'

'Scar killed her kid brother,' Joshua said. They turned and saw he was now on his feet and his eyes were clear. 'Know why?'

'Acosta raped his wife?'

'How'd you know that?'

'Just a lucky guess.'

Joshua gave Macahan a suspicious look but didn't say anything.

'It happened in the church minutes before my brother and Maria were to be married,' said Consuelo. 'Scar had tried to bed her many times before that, but always she would have nothing to do with him.'

'He had his men hold her down while he raped her in front of Paco's folks and all the guests,' Joshua said, 'When Paco tried to stop him, Acosta shot him in the legs. Then, after he was finished with Maria, he tied Paco behind his horse and dragged him around the plaza until he was dead.'

'Makes me sorry I killed the S.O.B. so fast,' Macahan said grimly. He added to Consuelo: 'Zach was wrong about you. Said you was keeping company with Scar's men. I'm sorry — '

'No need to apologize, *señor*. What your brother said is true. You see,' she added, 'much as I hated them to touch me I was hoping one day Scar would also want me and then when we were alone I would cut his evil throat and watch him die.'

25

Neither Macahan nor Joshua spoke during the ride back to camp. Both were buried deep in their thoughts; especially Joshua who, despite the beating, seemed to be feeling better emotionally. But after they had climbed the last hill and were riding along the deer trail that led to the camp fire, he suddenly reined up, forcing his brother to do the same.

'What's wrong?' Macahan asked.

'I need to know something before we get to camp.'

'Ask.'

'It's about Celia . . . '

For a moment, Macahan felt uneasy. 'Go on.'

'She told you what happened, didn't she?'

''Bout what?'

'Between her and that bastard Acosta.'

Macahan took the makings out of his pocket and patiently began to roll a smoke.

'Quit stalling, Ezra. Answer my question.'

'Not every question has an answer, *hermano*.'

'More stalling? What'd Celia do, make you promise not to tell me? It's all right,' he continued when Macahan didn't answer, 'I won't ask you to break your word. Not that you would, anyway.' He took the finished cigarette out of his brother's fingers, stuck it in his mouth, and dug around for a match.

'Here,' Macahan scratched a match on the horn, cupped his hands around the flame and leaned over so his brother could light up.

'Just tell me this. When we were talking before in Consuelo's place and you said Scar raped Maria — was that really a lucky guess?'

'What else?'

'I don't know. That's why I'm asking

you.' Joshua studied his brother, looking for answers in stone-gray eyes that told him nothing. 'For some reason I sensed you were trying to tell me something. Were you?'

'Reckon you'll have to decide that for yourself.'

Joshua thought long and hard before saying: 'I think I just did. Thanks . . . ' Returning the half-smoked cigarette to his brother, he spurred his horse on along the trail.

★   ★   ★

In camp Celia and the Apache sat talking beside the fire. They spoke softly so as not to awaken Daniel and when they heard horses approaching both stood up and looked anxiously at the two shadowy horsemen riding out of the darkness.

'*¡Madre de Dios!*' Celia said as she saw Joshua's bruised face. '*¿Que paso?*'

'I got into a fight.'

'Over what?'

'I'll tell you another time. Right now I've got something more important I want to talk to you about.'

'As you wish,' she said coldly.

'Here, I'll take those . . . ' Macahan took Joshua's reins and led both horses to the tether line. The Apache got the hint, and followed him, But as they unsaddled the horses, Macahan kept his eye on his brother in case he got out of hand.

Joshua rested his hands on his wife's shoulders and looked down into her dark, expressive eyes. He could see his reflection in them and behind him the moon, which seemed to be resting on his left shoulder.

'Why is it,' he said quietly, 'you could tell my brother what happened between you and Scar but you couldn't tell me — your husband?'

She returned his gaze unflinchingly. 'You never gave me a chance. You'd already decided what happened before I could explain.'

'Then you did intend to tell me?'

'Eventually. No, I take that back,' she said. 'I'm not sure. *Quizas.*'

'Maybe?'

'Maybe.'

'That's no answer.'

'It's the only one I have right now.'

'So in other words, you might not have ever told me?'

'It's possible. As I said, I'm not sure what I would have done. Not after the way you acted.'

'How was I supposed to act? I spend eight years believing Daniel is my son and then suddenly, seconds after my brother has been gunned down. I hear you saying he isn't — that the man who kidnapped him, the man who is responsible for Zach's death, the man we're all there to kill, is. I mean, that's kind of short notice to expect me to just laugh and shrug it off, don't you think?'

'I did not expect you to laugh or shrug it off.'

'What did you expect?'

'Shhhh. Lower your voice. You'll wake Daniel.'

'Well?' Joshua asked softly.

'I don't know what I expected. Right now I don't even know what to think. My head is in a spin. Tonight I went to sleep praying that tomorrow you and I and Daniel would find a way to stay together as a family, and I wake up in the middle of the night to discover you have run off to Janos — '

'I didn't 'run off.' I wanted a drink.'

'Whatever your reason, you weren't here. And I had no idea where you were. You could have been dead or lying in a ravine somewhere with a broken leg for all I knew. You could even have left me — us — and returned to Camp Furlong — '

'Lincoln knew where I went. He followed me.'

'And if he had been asleep or gone off to hunt with the wolf, what then?'

Joshua sighed, the exhaled air seeming to dispel all his anger. 'I'm sorry,' he said. 'You're right. It was a damned stupid thing to do — stupid and thoughtless. I just wasn't thinking straight. All I could think about was you with Scar and . . . ' his voice trailed off miserably.

For a long moment neither spoke. Somewhere in the nearby darkness an owl hooted. The sudden noise startled them back to reality.

'Do you have anything else to say to me?' Celia asked.

'N-No . . . ' Joshua paused, unable to find the words he wanted, then said: 'I just wanted you to know I knew about the rape and — '

'I have not yet said there *was* a rape.'

Joshua frowned. 'But I thought — '

'By my silence that I was agreeing with you?'

'Weren't you?'

'I wasn't agreeing or disagreeing.'

Joshua flushed. 'Dammit, Celia, what are you trying to tell me? That there never was a rape?'

'Would you forgive me if there wasn't?'

'No . . . I mean, I . . . I don't know. I'm not sure.'

'I see . . . ' Celia paused, fighting tears. 'Well, when you make up your mind, let me know. I have a son to raise, and I would like to know if he has a father or not.' Turning, she stormed off to her bedroll.

Joshua stared angrily after her. 'He's my son, too, you know.'

26

The long ride to the border was exhausting but uneventful. Not wanting to tax themselves or the horses in the relentless heat, they rode slowly but steadily, stopping in La Ascencion and El Milagro and various other villages along their route to eat and quench their thirst. A lighter mood prevailed almost everywhere they went. People were friendlier and more willing to speak to them than they had been previously — though the sight of the wolf trotting along behind the Apache made them keep their distance. Curious, Macahan asked Celia to talk to three *campesinos* toiling in a field outside La Viuda and see if she could find out what had caused the sudden turnaround. She spoke to one of the older men and was told that their good spirits were due to Pancho Villa's recent defeat at Columbus. Fearful of retaliation from the United States, Villa and his ragtag army had scattered into the Sierra Madre and no longer posed a threat to anyone — not even the few remaining wealthy *hacendados*.

'I don't get it,' Macahan said when Celia related what she'd learned. 'I thought Villa was revered in Chihuahua.'

'By some, yes, but not everyone. Especially now. People know he has lost the battle not only against the U.S., but Carranza too, and now fear that they will be singled out by the *Carrancistas* if they continue to align themselves with Villa.' She smiled ruefully. 'I'm afraid my people are famous for being — how is it we say in America — 'fair weather friends.' They are also a humble people, especially in the rural areas, who feel most comfortable when they are not involved in revolutionary chaos.'

'Who isn't?' said Joshua. It was the first time he'd spoken to Celia since they had broken camp. 'Even in the dog days of summer there isn't anyone at Camp Furlong who wouldn't rather get drunk in El Paso than go off to war.'

Celia made no attempt to respond or look at him and Joshua once again lapsed into gloomy silence. They rode on, crossing the ever-curving *Rio Casas Grandes* just north of Los Efrain and then resting on the opposite bank before starting the final leg through the desert to Palomas.

As if anxious to keep herself separated from Joshua, Celia helped the Apache feed and water the horses; while Daniel sat with his uncle and father under the trees. He too had been unusually quiet during the ride but now as he watched them rolling their cigarettes, he asked his Uncle Ezra if one day he would teach him how to roll his own. 'Sure,' Macahan said. 'Be happy to. Remind me next time I'm in Columbus.'

'When will that be?'

'Whenever his work brings him

there,' Joshua said.

Daniel looked disappointed.

'If that ain't soon enough for you,' Macahan said. 'Have your pa show you.'

'He doesn't roll them as tight as you do,' Daniel said. 'I tried one of his already and the tobacco kept falling out.'

'Why do you think I went to readyrolls,' Joshua said. 'Got tired of wasting good tobacco.'

'Fella has to keep practicing,' Macahan said. 'Though I reckon there are some men, no matter how hard they try, just don't have the knack. To me now, it just came natural.'

'How old were you when you first started smoking, Uncle Ezra?'

'About your age, boy. Maybe a tad younger.' Macahan grinned and tousled Daniel's thick black curls. 'I use to steal 'em from your Grampa Zane when he wasn't looking. He kept a whole parcel of smokes already rolled in an old coffee can in his study; said he liked the

way they smelled after they had been in
the can for a spell. 'Course, that wasn't
really the reason. The truth was he had
a severe case of the shakes — '

'From whiskey, you mean?'

'Uh-uh. Some kind of illness that
come over him when he got older.
Finally got so bad he couldn't roll his
own smokes or hold a glass without
spilling whatever was in it.'

'Palsy,' said Joshua.

'What?'

'Grampa Zane's illness — that's what
it's called: palsy.'

Macahan arched his dark, graying
eyebrows. 'Learn something every day.
See how smart your pa is,' he said to
Daniel. 'That's why you got to keep
going to school and doing your
book-learning. Otherwise, you'll end up
thick between the ears like your Uncle
Ezra.'

Daniel giggled. 'You're a U.S. marshal,' he said, 'you can't be thick
between the ears. Can he, Dad?'

Joshua shook his head. 'He just likes

to pretend he is, so he can surprise people when he does something smart. Like learning how to draw birds and imitating their calls.'

'Oh, Judas, no,' Macahan began. But he was too late.

'Birds?' Daniel said, his tone making Macahan cringe. 'You draw *birds*, Uncle Ezra?'

'I'm trying to, yeah. Pretty sissy hobby, huh?'

Daniel shrugged. 'If I was a marshal I'd be practicing how to shoot straighter or draw faster.'

'He can already do those things better than most,' Joshua said. 'This is for later, after all the gunmen and outlaws are gone and he retires.' He frowned, troubled by his thoughts, then said: 'Wish to God I had a talent or hobby to fall back on. I'd be out of this man's army quicker than you can wink.'

'Not me,' said Daniel. Rising, he picked up a flat stone and threw it into the slow-flowing river. The stone skipped across the surface and then sunk with a faint plop. 'If I was a U.S. Marshal I'd never retire.'

'Never's a long time,' Macahan said.

'I don't care. I'd keep on doing it until I killed off all the outlaws and everybody said I was the greatest marshal ever lived. And then I'd travel about the country talking about how I won all these gunfights and maybe I'd even have a Wild West show like Buffalo Bill Cody. You know, with lots of Injuns chasing stagecoaches and me leading the cavalry to the rescue.'

'Good Lord,' Joshua said. 'Where do you get such wild notions?'

'I'd never retire if I was a soldier either,' Daniel said. 'I'd stay until I was a famous general and then I'd ride my white horse in parades and order everybody around and go to the White House where the President would give me all these medals and tell everyone how brave I was.'

'Sounds like you got your life all mapped out,' Macahan said.

'What's wrong with that?'

'Nothing if it works. Unfortunately,' Joshua said, 'things don't always work out how we planned them.'

'They would if folks didn't keep on retiring before they got what they wanted.' He threw another stone into the river. This one sunk immediately. Clearly disgusted, Daniel ran off and joined his mother and the Apache.

Macahan grinned. 'Too bad he's so shy.'

'He gets his confidence from his mother,' Joshua said. 'She thinks she can move mountains and most times, she can.'

Macahan chose his words carefully. 'Celia's a fine woman. No doubt about that. But maybe you ain't giving yourself enough credit.'

'Meaning?'

'It wasn't Celia who volunteered to break Zach out of jail. It wasn't Celia who was willing to go AWOL to rescue his son. And it sure as hell wasn't Celia who risked his life to save me when I was trapped by that burning net while

Scar's men were trying to shoot you with machine guns.'

'You'd of done the same for me.'

'I like to think so. I try not to run scared and to earn my wages, but believe me there's plenty of times I took the safe road home.'

'Really?'

'Got my word on it.'

There was silence as Joshua mulled over his brother's words.

'Thanks for telling me that, Ez.'

'Just wanted you to know you ain't alone when it comes to doubting yourself.' Rising, Macahan stretched the stiffness from his back and flipped his butt into the river. 'Well, if we're going to make Columbus 'fore dark, we better get rollin'.'

'I'll tell the others.'

'Josh, wait . . . '

Joshua turned and looked back at his brother. 'What?'

'I'm proud of you, *hermano*. And if Zach was alive, he'd be proud of you, too.'

Joshua didn't say anything. But as he watched Macahan walking to the horses, he realized that for one of the few times in his life he didn't feel alone or lonely or without purpose.

27

It was dusk when they reached the border.
The guard outside the gate-shack remembered Macahan and nodded curtly. He
was about to wave them on through
when he saw the wolf crouched behind
the Apache. He jumped back in alarm.

'Hey! Ain't that a — a wolf?'

'Where?' said Macahan.

'Right there,' pointed the guard.

'You mean my dog?'

'Dog be damned. That's a wolf.
Anybody can tell that.'

'Well, 'anybody' would be wrong.
Sam's a dog. He just looks like a wolf.'

'Sure as hell does.'

'That's why he's called a wolfdog,'
the Apache said.

'Mean he's half dog and half wolf?'

'More like a smidgen wolf,' Macahan
said.

'Nearly all dog,' the Apache said.

'Well you could've fooled me,' said the guard. Eyes never leaving the wolf, he cautiously opened the gate. 'Wait,' he said as they started to move forward. 'Let me get inside first. I don't want to be bitten by no wolfdog.' He hurried into his gate-shack and waved at them through the window to go ahead.

They rode on through and up the Deming-Guzman road. Macahan looked back and saw the guard watching them and scratching his head.

'Uncle Ezra?'

'Yes, Dan'l?'

'Why'd you lie to that man?'

'Wasn't exactly a lie.'

'But you said he wasn't a wolf, and he is.'

'It's what you call a white lie.'

'What kind of lie is that?'

'One which everybody benefits from.'

'I don't understand.'

'Well, Uncle Lincoln benefits by getting his wolf across and the guard, he benefits because I don't have to shoot him.'

'He's just joking,' Joshua said as Daniel looked shocked. 'Uncle Ezra wouldn't really have shot him.' They rode on.

After three miles they reached Camp Furlong. Ahead, across the railroad tracks, peace and quiet had returned to Columbus. The little town was dark save for the lights in stores and houses. Very few people were on the streets and all that remained of the Commercial Hotel was a large patch of charred earth.

Macahan reined up. 'You three go on ahead,' he told Celia, Daniel, and the Apache. 'Josh and me, we'll be along later, soon as we get through visiting with Colonel Slocum.'

Celia gave Joshua a long, questioning look. 'Will you be spending the night at the base?'

'Not if I'm welcome at home.'

She studied him with her flashing dark eyes. 'Are you sure that's what you want?'

'More than anything,' Joshua said.

'Then I'll see what I can fix for supper.'

'Thanks. Anything you rustle up will do.' He leaned sideways in the saddle and fondly tousled his Daniel's hair. 'See you in a while, son.'

'Promise you'll be home to tuck me in?'

'Promise.' He watched as the Apache escorted Celia and Daniel across the tracks; then he turned to his brother and shrugged. 'It's a start.'

'First step's always the hardest,' Macahan said. He and Joshua kicked up their horses and rode into Camp Furlong. In the week or so since the raid, the camp had grown three times its original size. Hundreds of tents to house the trainloads of troops arriving daily from Ft. Bliss were now pitched on both sides of the road, and thousands of additional soldiers, arms and supplies were due before the end of the month.

At company headquarters Colonel Slocum was too busy to see them right away, and a pile of cigarette butts lay around their boots by the time they actually got to face him. He looked weary from his extra hours on duty, but he was excited about the fact that at last Washington had decided to act against Villa. 'The President's finally seen the light, gentlemen. He's ordered General Pershing to cross the border and capture that damned bandit.'

'I don't envy him,' Macahan said. 'Other than the Tarahumara, Villa knows the Sierra Madre better than anyone. He won't be easy to find.'

'Maybe not,' Colonel Slocum said. 'But General Pershing will have ten thousand men under his command, and he intends to scour every inch of those mountains. Trust me, gentlemen, with Black Jack himself leading the charge, Pancho Villa's days are numbered. Now, Corporal,' he added, his tone softening, 'regarding your son, I hope you have good news for me.'

'I do, sir.' Joshua quickly explained

that Daniel was safely back home and that Acosta and most of his men were dead.

'Wonderful. That is good news.'

'Not all of it,' Macahan said grimly. 'We buried our brother.'

'Lt. Macahan's dead?'

Macahan nodded.

'What happened?'

'Zach was talking to Scar, trying to make a swap for Daniel. Bastard never gave him a chance. Had his men gun him down, cold.'

'Damn. What a loss! But you did kill Scar?'

Macahan nodded and tapped his forefinger between his eyes. 'Happy to say I pulled the trigger myself.'

'It was long overdue.' Colonel Slocum paused and wearily squeezed his brow. 'I'm truly sorry to hear about your brother. He was a fine officer. As brave as they come.'

Macahan and Joshua exchanged looks, surprised by the colonel's praise.

'I'm glad you feel that way,' Macahan

said, 'because I'd like to ask you a favor.'

'What sort of favor?'

'Well, since Zach is dead and can't cause you no more trouble, I was wondering if you'd consider wiping his slate clean.'

Colonel Slocum stared at Macahan, unable to believe his gall. 'Are you suggesting what I think you're suggesting — that I strike the fact that your brother was a deserter from his record?'

'Well, he did give his life in the line of duty, Colonel.'

'Rescuing his nephew from a Mexican brigand, though courageous, hardly qualifies as a military campaign.'

'Maybe not. But Zach believed that what he was taught at West Point prepared him for the rest of his life. That should count for something.'

'We know he wasn't a model soldier,' Joshua added, 'and that his attitude was often in conflict with his superiors, but . . . without Zach, my wife and I wouldn't have our son back. And we'll always love him for that, sir.'

Colonel Slocum absently stroked his mustache as he absorbed Joshua's words. Rising, he clasped his hands behind his back and stared out the window at the darkening twilight. He seemed to be pondering something and after a few moments he sighed, resigned, and turned back to Macahan and Joshua. 'Suppose I told you your brother wasn't a deserter?'

'Sir?'

'What if I said he was a spy for the Army, a young man willing to throw away his good name and a brilliant career in order to serve his country?'

'*Is* that what you're saying?' Macahan said.

Colonel Slocum's expression indicated that he was.

'So this was all a charade so Zach could pretend he was a Villista?'

'More than just a Villista, gentlemen. Lt. Macahan's orders were to spy on the German legation; to get information about their infiltration into Mexican politics — and, specifically, Carranza's corrupt government. Which, I might add, he did most admirably.'

The brothers Macahan could only stand there in shocked silence.

'And you knew this all along?' Macahan said finally.

Colonel Slocum's eyes said yes, he did. But at the same time he frowned and said: 'Knew what?'

'Ah-huh,' Macahan said.

Joshua, not catching on, said: 'You must've known, Colonel, or you wouldn't have helped Zach escape from jail.'

Colonel Slocum looked blankly at him. 'Corporal, I have no idea what you're talking about.'

'Sure you do. You just said — '

'What's more,' the colonel interrupted, 'I'm sure no one else in this regiment — or in the entire Army for that matter — would know, either.'

'I bet they wouldn't,' Macahan said.

The colonel ignored him. 'So I advise both of you never to mention the matter again. Because if you try to pursue this idiotic notion, it would only make matters worse in regards to Lt. Macahan's military record. Do I make myself clear, gentlemen?'

'Amen, brother,' Macahan said, sounding just like Zachary.

Colonel Slocum gave the lawman a withering look. 'Marshal, I would tread very lightly from now on. Forging the signature of a commanding officer in order to steal Army supplies is sufficient cause to have you thrown in the stockade for a very long time. Is *that* clear?'

'Yes, sir.'

'Splendid.' Colonel Slocum turned to Joshua. 'Due to our upcoming campaign against Villa, Corporal, your furlough is officially over. You are to report back here by reveille, ready and willing to serve your country.'

'Yes, sir.'

'Hang on,' Macahan said. 'You sure you know what you're doing, *hermano?*'

'Absolutely.' Joshua looked at Colonel Slocum. 'I know I've been a thorn in your side, sir, but from now on you can count on me. I won't let you down.'

'I never thought you would, son.' Colonel Slocum gave a rare smile. 'It might interest you to know, Corporal, that none other than General Ulysses S. Grant himself often questioned his desire to be a soldier.'

'I didn't know that, sir.'

'Few people do. But it merely proves what I've stated all along: not every acorn knows it's destined to be an oak.' Turning to Macahan, he added: 'As for you, Marshal — you are to return everything you 'borrowed' from this base and then never set foot on it again.'

'That might be a problem, Colonel.'

'In what way?'

'Well, I'd like to oblige you, but the mule and the bay are dead and the ammo and supplies all used up, so there really ain't nothing to return.'

Colonel Slocum swallowed, hard. 'Very well. Dismissed.' He returned Joshua's salute then sat behind his desk and continued with his paperwork. He seemed to be immersed in his work. But as Macahan and Joshua reached the door, he spoke softly and without looking up.

'Good work, gentlemen.'

Joshua started to turn around but Macahan grabbed his arm and pushed him out the door.

'Why'd you do that?' Joshua asked as they walked to their horses. 'We should've at least thanked him.'

'Like hell,' said Macahan. 'That'd be like thanking the hangman for not dropping the trap. Next thing you know he's had second thoughts and *wham* — you're dangling with your feet off the ground.'

28

They rode home in empty-hearted silence. Insects whined about their ears in the cool darkness. The horses' hooves thudded monotonously on the flat dusty road. Out in the desert coyotes began their nightly chorus. Neither Macahan nor Joshua heard anything. They were lost in their thoughts, each reliving his favorite memory of their departed brother.

The moon now came from behind the clouds silhouetting the two brothers against the distant horizon. Ahead, to the west, the mountains known as the *Tres Hermanas* appeared to be huddled closer together than usual, as if the Three Sisters were afraid they, like the Macahans, might lose one of their own.

When the brothers dismounted by the corral behind Joshua's house, they found the Apache stripped to the waist splitting wood for the stove. He was using his kukri and with each downward chop the big curved blade gleamed in the moonlight. Pausing to open the gate for them, he looked at Macahan with a needling grin.

'I didn't expect to see you so soon.'

'Figured I'd be in the stockade, huh?'

'It seemed like a reasonable conclusion.'

'Sorry to disappoint you, *amigo*.'

'Colonel Slocum did kick him off the base, though,' said Joshua.

'He did no such thing. He just said I could never come back.'

'Same thing. Not that it matters. With all the troop movements and supplies coming into camp right now, he's probably already forgotten he said it.' Unsaddling his horse, Joshua threw the saddle and blanket over the fence. 'You'll never guess what else he said, Linc. Tell him, Ez. Tell him what the C.O. said about Zach not being a deserter.'

Briefly, Macahan repeated everything

the Colonel had told them.

The Apache's stoic expression never changed.

'You don't seem too surprised,' Joshua said.

'It makes sense.'

'It does? How?'

'While he was in Mexico with Villa your brother would occasionally show up at my cabin. When he did, he'd bring bottles of brandy and tequila and we would talk long into the night.'

'I didn't know that,' Joshua said. 'Did you know that, Ezra?'

'Finish what you're saying,' Macahan said to the Apache.

'I sensed he was a man whose feet took him where he did not want to go.'

'Don't talk in riddles, dammit.'

'Zach told me once he'd become a deserter because the Army was too restrictive and he wanted to enjoy life. I asked him if he ever regretted his decision. He laughed and said hell no, he was too busy having fun to regret anything. But when he wasn't drinking or talking about the women he'd bedded, I could tell he was very lonely and sad and I knew there had to be a logical reason for it.'

'Then you knew more than us,' Joshua said. 'Both Ezra and I never questioned it for a moment.'

'That's because we grew up with him,' Macahan said. 'Knew what he was like. Hell, never a day went by that Zach wasn't in some kind of hot water.'

'We still should have given him the benefit of the doubt. He was our brother. And I'll go to my grave wishing I could tell him I'm sorry for believing he could be a deserter.' Overcome with emotion, Joshua slammed into the house.

'He's really hurting,' Lincoln said.

'Comes from wearing his heart on his sleeve,' said Macahan. 'I keep telling him not to do it, but he won't listen.'

'Least he has a heart.'

'I don't?'

'Debatable.'

'I'll dig it up and show you — soon

as I retire.' Macahan suddenly remembered the wolf and looked around.
'*¿Donde esta el Señor Lobo?*'

The Apache thumbed in the direction of the desert. 'Introducing himself
to the local wildlife, last I heard.'

'Hopefully that'll keep his mind off
the horses.'

Lincoln went on splitting wood. 'You
thinking of keeping the gray?'

'Uh-uh. Josh is goin' to sell him to
one of the officers for me.'

'I thought you liked that horse?'

'I do. But he's way too good to waste
on what I'd use him for. Purebred like
him, he deserves to be prancing at the
head of a parade, not chasing some
woolly-assed jasper willing to shoot him
just to get me off his trail. How about
you?' Macahan added. 'Are you taking
the wolf with you to the reservation?'

'I'd like to, but I could never get him
onto the train.'

'Be fun to see you try.'

'Be fun to see him bite me, you
mean.'

Macahan chuckled. 'What do you think will happen to him?'

'Once he realizes I am gone, he'll head back across the border.'

'He'll be better off there. He stays here, a rancher will shoot him for the bounty; 'least in Chihuahua he can roam free for a spell before some Mex traps him, sells his hide, and cooks him up with chili.'

The Apache shot him a sour look. 'Macahan, you are one cold-hearted son of a bitch.'

'So I've been told.' Taking two cigars from his pocket, Macahan tossed one to the Apache.

Lincoln held it to his nose and grimaced. 'Where did you get these?'

'From the station-master when I bought our tickets. All the stores were shuttered, and I was in desperate need of a cigar.'

'I am not that desperate.'

'Then why are you putting it in your pocket?'

'For when I *am* that desperate.'

'We can always buy cigars on the train. Never knowed a conductor yet on the midnight run who didn't keep a box just for that very purpose.'

The Apache began gathering up the split wood. 'I will miss the boy,' he said presently.

'Me, too. Good kid. Josh and Celia should be proud of themselves.'

'Maybe he will be the resin that helps keep them together.'

'Be pretty to think so.' Macahan bit the end off his cigar, flared a match, and lit the tip. The first puff made him grimace; the second made him curse and hurl the cigar off into the darkness. 'The fella who rolled that ought to be shot,' he said. Swatting away a mosquito whining in his ear, he added: 'Think you'll ever have young'uns of your own?'

'No.'

'Why not? You ain't that ugly. Must be some squaw willing to put up with you.'

'Macahan, I can't even teach a wolf

not to eat my horse, what kind of father would I make?'

'Good point.'

'You?'

'Not if Texas falls into the Gulf.'

'What does that mean exactly? — 'if Texas falls in the Gulf'?'

'Beats me.'

'You say it all the time.'

'I like the way it sounds.'

'Hey, Ezra — ' Joshua stuck his head out the door. 'Supper's on the table. You, too,' he said to Lincoln. 'Better look sharp. Celia doesn't like the food to get cold.'

'He ain't finished his chores yet — *hey*!' Macahan jumped up as the kukri buried in the stump between his legs. 'You dumb loco Injun, any closer and I'd be talking like a choirboy.'

'Sorry, Macahan.' The Apache pulled the big knife out of the stump. 'It slipped out of my hands.'

'Like hell it did,' Macahan said. But he was grinning as he said it, and so were Joshua and the Apache. They entered the house pushing and punching each other like playful schoolboys. The door closed behind them, shutting out the long triumphant howl of a wolf that had just made a successful kill.

THE END

We do hope that you have enjoyed reading this large print book.

Did you know that all of our titles are available for purchase?

We publish a wide range of high quality large print books including:
Romances, Mysteries, Classics
General Fiction
Non Fiction and Westerns

Special interest titles available in large print are:
The Little Oxford Dictionary
Music Book, Song Book
Hymn Book, Service Book

Also available from us courtesy of Oxford University Press:
Young Readers' Dictionary
(large print edition)
Young Readers' Thesaurus
(large print edition)

For further information or a free brochure, please contact us at:
Ulverscroft Large Print Books Ltd.,
The Green, Bradgate Road, Anstey,
Leicester, LE7 7FU, England.
Tel: (00 44) **0116 236 4325**
Fax: (00 44) **0116 234 0205**

TWO GUN MARSHAL

John Saunders

Packing two guns, Jeff Bellamy comes to Red Rock to help his father's best friend, but finds Dorlen beyond help, and a town dying because its freight lines are being ruined. Tough man Bellamy dislikes small-timers being pushed around, so he stays. And, when the crooked marshal drops to a well-aimed bullet, takes over his job. But Red Rock comes perilously closer to its demise before its new marshal gets to grips with the instigator of all the trouble.

HIGH MOUNTAIN STAND-OFF

John C. Danner

The only thing Sam Harper knew about himself was his skill with a gun. His past was a blank, his future unknown. Then he met the beautiful and wealthy Virginia Maitland whose life was under threat from unseen enemies — she desperately needed his help to find answers. Together they rode a dangerous trail, battling the raging elements as well as their would-be assassins. Only the crash of gunfire would determine the outcome in a final showdown.